What *IS THAT*?

Okay, our ranch crew was in the process of receiving one of the most humiliating defeats in history. We had set out on a simple task, to load a bull, and the bull had ended up loading us.

I was embarrassed. Loper was mad. Slim was beyond mad. But then something really strange happened. A big yellow Labrador retriever stumbled out of some wild plum thickets on the south side of the road, and—this is the most amazing part, so pay attention—on his head he was wearing a BIRD CAGE!

I'm not kidding. A bird cage!

Slim was the first to see it. "Good honk, what IS THAT?"

Loper squinted his eyes and looked. I squinted my eyes and looked. Neither of us could believe what we were seeing. But here's the best part: the bull couldn't believe it either.

The Case of the Perfect Dog

John R. Erickson

Illustrations by Gerald L. Holmes

Maverick Books, Inc.

Eri

MAVERICK BOOKS, INC.
Published by Maverick Books, Inc.
P.O. Box 549, Perryton, TX 79070
Phone: 806.435.7611
www.hankthecowdog.com

First published in the United States of America by Maverick Books, Inc. 2012.

1 3 5 7 9 10 8 6 4 2

LIBRARY OF CONGRESS CONTROL NUMBER: 2012931090

978-1-59188-159-9 (paperback); 978-1-59188-259-6 (hardcover)

Hank the Cowdog® is a registered trademark of John R. Erickson.

Printed in the United States of America

To Tim and Lyndsay Lambert
of the Texas Home School Coalition

CONTENTS

CHAPTER ONE

Another Grinding Day in the Office

It's me again, Hank the Cowdog. The mystery began one day in August. Yes, it was August because oftentimes in August, the wind quits blowing and we have water problems on the ranch. See, when the wind quits blowing, the windmills don't turn and the cattle run out of water in the stock tanks.

When you're operating a ranch in the Texas Panhandle, the one thing you can't do in the summertime is run out of water. Cattle can live for weeks without feed, but let 'em run out of water and they start dropping dead. That has never happened on this ranch, but only because...

Actually, that water business came up later in the week, so forget that I brought it up. The day

1

of which we are speaking began as most days begin—in the morning. All our days follow a regular schedule, don't you see. We have morning, then afternoon, then evening, then night, and it doesn't matter whether it is raining or Tuesday.

On that particular morning, Little Alfred came out of the house around ten o'clock. The slamming of the screen door woke me up.

Wait. Let's rephrase that. I'm never in bed at that hour of the morning, so I couldn't have been awakened by the slamming of the screen door. I was at my desk, doing paperwork and going over a stack of reports. As usual, I'd gotten about three hours of sleep. I mean, the work never ends on this ranch: night patrol, Monster Watch, Bark at the Mailman, coyote alerts, and taking care of the kids. We squeeze in a few hours of gunnysack time when we can.

So, yes, I was at my desk, and heard the slamming of the screen door. Drover, my assistant, heard it too, and said, "Sniffle tricky turnip blooms on the back door piffle."

I looked up from the report I was reading. "Hardly ever murky snap foggy bottoms."

"Red suspenders?"

"I agree, or donkey underpants in the green tomatoes."

We stared into each other's eyes for a long moment, then Drover said, "Oh, hi. Did you just wake up?"

"Absolutely not. I've been acroak for hours." I glanced around. "Where are we?"

"When?"

"I'm not sure, right now, I guess."

"Well," he yawned, "I'd say we're still in bed."

"Rubbish. It's almost noon." I leaped to my feet and took a step...and fell on my face. "Where did I put my legs last night?"

"Well, I think you're still wearing them."

"In that case, they're not working properly. Have you been tampering with my legs?"

"I think you're still asleep. Try 'em again."

"Please don't tell me what to do." I rose to my feet and took several steps. "Okay, they're working now."

"See? You were asleep."

"I was not asleep." I narrowed my eyes and studied the dog to whom I was speaking. "Wait a second, who are you?"

"I'm Drover, remember me?"

"Oh yes, it's coming back to me now. We used to work together, right?"

"Still do."

3

I gave him a hard look. "If we work together, why are you still in bed at this hour of the morning?"

"Well…"

"Five demerits for slacking."

"Yeah, but…"

"Ten demerits."

"You were in bed too."

"Fifteen demerits and three Chicken Marks." At that moment, I heard the squeaking of a gate. "Drover, I don't want to alarm you, but we have an unidentified person or persons on the ranch."

"Yeah, it's Little Alfred. He just came out of the house."

"Oh? Why wasn't I informed? How can I run this ranch when nobody turns in their reports?"

He heaved a sigh. "Hank, you were asleep."

I marched over to him and melted him with a glare. "Stand at attention when I'm addressing you."

He stiffened his posture and sat up straight. "Sorry."

"This outfit has no more discipline than a pack of stray cats."

"Meow."

"I beg your pardon?"

"I said, yeah."

"What ever happened to 'Yes Sir'?"

"Sorry. Yes sir."

I began pacing in front of him. I mean, he was fixing to get the full load. "I was not asleep, and spreading lies about a superior officer is a serious offense. If it happens again, you will spend entire days and nights with your nose in the corner."

"I said I was sorry."

"Hush. Nobody cares if you're sorry."

"Okay, I'm not sorry."

"The trouble with you is that you're never sorry for your mistakes."

"Sorry."

"It's your attitude, Drover. You have a lousy attitude. I ought to throw the book at you, but I'm going to let you off easy this time. Twenty-three demerits and fifteen Chicken Marks."

"Ouch."

"Don't argue with me. This will go into your permanent record."

"Thanks."

"You're dismissed." I glanced around. "What were we doing before you provoked this outburst?"

"Well, let me think." He rolled his eyes. "Oh yeah, Little Alfred just came out of the house."

"In that case, we haven't a moment to spare. Prepare to launch all dogs!"

And with that, we dived into our Rocket Dog suits and went streaking through ranch headquarters to join our little pal. We had no idea what he was doing, but among the possibilities was that he had come out of the house with breakfast scraps, and you know where I stand on that issue.

Scrap Time is a major event in the life of every dog. Not only do we enjoy wolfing down the scraps, but we draw even more pleasure wolfing at the cat and making sure that he gets no scraps. Hee, hee.

Yes, by George, we needed to check this out.

We arrived just as the boy was coming out the yard gate. I reconoodled the situation, and noted that he carried a red plastic bucket in his right hand. Left hand. He was carrying a bucket, is the point, and it really doesn't matter which hand was doing the work. The real question was—what did the bucket contain?

See, at our previous Scrap Events, he had come outside with a plate and a fork, not a bucket. Most of the time, the plate held luscious scraps and he used the fork to scrape them off the plate, at which point we dogs did our best job of gobbling them down...while following certain anti-cat procedures, shall we say.

May I speak frankly about those procedures? They're designed to encourage our little creep of a cat to move along. His name is Pete. We don't like him and we're dedicated to the belief that he deserves no scraps, none, zero. Any time Pete gets a bite of scraps, we regard it as a personal tragedy for our side. It plunges the entire Security Division into a period of mourning and brooding.

Why should the cat receive the reward of scraps? He does nothing that contributes to the good of the ranch. On an average day, he spends most of his time lurking in the iris patch. Now and then, he will come out to rub on someone's ankles or to whine for a handout, but you'll never see him doing what ranch cats are supposed to do: catching mice. That's too much trouble. He makes me sick.

But would you like to guess who followed Little Alfred out the gate? Mister Never Sweat, Mister Kitty Moocher. His mere presence caused lights to flash in the control room of my mind, and I heard a fearsome rumble in the depths of my throat.

I rolled up to him and lifted Tooth Shields, revealing two rows of bad news for cats. "Get lost, kitty, dogs are on the scene. Buzz off, go back to your spider web."

Do you suppose he took the hint? Oh no. Cats don't take hints. He gave me his usual smirk, and in his usual whiney voice, he said, "My, my! I think the cops have just arrived."

"You get a bingo on that. The cops are here and the cats need to move along. Scram."

"But Hankie, I'm curious to see what's in the red bucket."

"What's in the red bucket is classified information. You'll be told after we've checked it out."

"But Hankie," he widened his eyes, "what if it contains scraps?"

"We'll make that announcement at the appropriate time, after we've had a chance to sift through the material. If we find scraps, you'll never see them, but we might tell you about them." I turned to my assistant. "Drover, stand by. We might need to help this cat find a tree."

Drover giggled. "Oh goodie, this'll be fun!" Drover must have been feeling brave, because he inched closer to the cat and growled. "Pick a tree, Pete, 'cause we're fixing to..."

Bam! It was a left jab. It came out of nowhere and left a tattoo on the soft leathery portion of Drover's nose. He never saw it coming, and let out a squall of shock and pain. By then, it was over. Pete high-balled it back to the yard and took up a position right below Sally May's kitchen window. From that location, he waved a paw and stuck out his tongue at us.

Pete had just brought us to the drink of war.

The *brink* of war.

CHAPTER TWO

A Non-Scrap Event

Drover was stunned. "He hit me and I hadn't even done anything yet. Now look at him! He's sticking out his tongue at us."

"I understand, son, but we have to let this one go. We can't risk sending troops into the yard. Don't forget Sally May and her broom."

"Yeah, but he slugged me!"

"I know he did, but let me point out something very important. Pete's gone and we've got the scraps all to ourselves. That's what we wanted, right?"

"Yeah, but my nose hurts."

"Son, you were brave. You accomplished your mission, you got rid of a nuisance, and I'm proud of you."

He stared at me, then smiled. "You are?"

I gave him a pat on the shoulder. "Absolutely, and you know what else? I think we can forget about those demerits and Chicken Marks. Let's just say they disappeared from our files. Now, let's check out the scraps."

"What about my nose?"

"Bring it along. You can use it on the scraps."

It isn't often that Drover distinguishes himself in combat, and when he does, we try to make a big deal out of it. I realize that getting sucker-punched by a cat isn't the highest form of bravery, but at least the little guy had dared to put his nose into harm's way. It was a start, and maybe it would give us something to build on.

After that touching ceremony, we turned our attention to...where was the boy? And, more to the point, where was that bucket of scraps? He'd been right there beside us when the fighting had broken out, but now...

At last I caught sight of him. He had gone to the garden, a patch of fertile ground that had been enclosed inside a hog wire fence. You might say that we dogs were not encouraged to go there. Why? Sally May had some peculiar ideas about dogs and gardens. On the few rare occasions when we had jumped the fence, our presence had caused major explosions.

So it struck me as odd that Alfred had chosen to do Scrap Distribution in the garden. He was about to enter the gate when we arrived on the scene, out of breath but glowing with anticipation of the big event.

Right away, I went into the Loyal Dog Waiting Configuration: plopped my hind quarters on the ground, sat at attention, and beamed him Looks of Longing and Sincerity. Drover followed my lead and did the same.

The boy seemed surprised. "Hi Hankie, what do you want?"

Well...uh...at the risk of seeming blunt...what was in the bucket?

"Oh, you want some skwaps?"

Well, sure, scraps would be nice. Yes, absolutely. I gave my tail five vigorous thumps on the ground.

He shrugged. "Sorry, I took out the skwaps right after breakfast, and you weren't there."

Huh?

"I gave 'em all to Pete." He pointed to the bucket. "This is stuff for the compost heap."

WHAT! Compost heap! He'd given all the breakfast scraps to that miserable little...my mind was swirling. In the distance, I heard the

13

cat laughing his head off.

I turned to my assistant. "We've been tricked."

"You mean...I got slugged for nothing?"

"Yes, that's exactly what it means. Pete lured us into an argument over scraps that don't exist. He ate them two hours ago."

"Oh darn, now I'm all upset."

"Fool! How could you have fallen for Pete's treachery?"

"Gosh, what did I do?"

"Well, in the first place...Drover, Life is full of details. The fact that I can't remember them doesn't mean they don't exist."

"Pete got the scraps 'cause we slept late. That's the reason you're mad."

"That's one of the reasons I'm mad. The other is that you're still spreading lies and gossip about your commanding officer—namely, that I slept late."

"Yeah, but it's true."

"All right, then you're spreading *truth* about your commanding officer and that's even worse."

"Yeah, but you gave me an award for bravery."

"I'm glad you mentioned that. The award has been revoked and those Chicken Marks are going right back on your record."

He gave me a wounded look. "Yeah, but I

didn't do anything wrong!"

"Drover, the cat is laughing his head off and one of us has to accept the blame. I could take the blame, but think of the effect it would have on morale of this outfit."

He blinked his eyes. "Gosh, I never thought of that."

"It could be devastating. Here's the solution. You take the blame, go to your room, and stick your nose in the corner for five minutes. That will put an end to the whole nasty episode."

"That doesn't sound so bad."

I whopped him on the back. "I like your spirit, son. Now, run along and let's put this thing behind us."

"Okay, here I go!"

With an air of fatherly pride, I watched as he...huh? You know what he did? After running about ten steps toward the gas tanks, he made a hard right turn and highballed it straight to the machine shed, where he dived through the slot between the big sliding doors.

"Drover, this is the voice of your commanding officer! Return to base at once and put your nose in the corner! Drover?"

He had vanished into the depths of his Secret Sanctuary, and it would have taken a pack of

15

bloodhounds to find him in there.

You know, it breaks my heart when these things happen. You drill the men, try to teach them discipline and loyalty, and just when you think a light has come on in their tiny minds, they make a dumb decision and blow the whole thing to smithereens.

Oh well. We have to trudge on with our lives.

Little Alfred had dumped the contents of his bucket into the compost pit, so I drifted over to check it out. Sniff sniff. Carrot peelings, wilted lettuce, coffee grounds, onion skins, peach seeds, watermelon rinds, and three dozen potatoes that had sprouted in the pantry and gone bad. In other words, I was looking at vegetable garbage that a normal dog wouldn't touch, even if he was starving to death.

Yes, this had turned into a dark day on the ranch, and to make things even worse, I could hear Sally May's rotten little cat: "How are the scraps, Hankie? Hee, hee, hee!"

Right then and there, I made an entry in the Log Book of My Mind: "Kitty will pay for this." Exactly when and where he would pay had not been determined.

I turned to Little Alfred, my dearest pal in the world, gave him Shattered Looks and went to

Slow Wags on the tail section, as if to say, "Here's a thought. What are the chances that you could slip into the house and, you know, bring me a cookie? One little cookie might really turn things around."

No sale. He ordered me out of the garden and headed back to the house with his empty bucket. (Here's an important detail: he forgot to close the garden gate. That will come up later, so remember it).

At that very moment, I heard a vehicle pulling into ranch headquarters, and, well, you know me. Even when my heart is aching for breakfast scraps and cookies that never appear, I'm still Head of the ranch's Security Division, and I have to work Traffic.

Who else would do it? Drover? Pete? That's a laugh. Rain or shine, day or night, happy or sad, they can be counted on to do nothing. I have to rise to the occasion and monitor the comings and goings of all vehicles that enter my territory, and that's what I did. I went to Turbo Four on all engines and met the UV (Unidentified Vehicle) as it was coming down that little hill in front of the house.

Okay, false alarm. It was one of our ranch pickups, and it was pulling a sixteen-foot stock trailer. The driver was Slim Chance, the hired hand on this outfit. In other words, I didn't need to check his papers or run his license plate number through Data Control. I waved him through Security and gave him an escort down to the corrals. (When they're pulling a trailer, we know their destination: the corrals).

Loper had just turned the horses out into the pasture and made his appearance as Slim was backing the trailer up to the loading chute. When Slim stepped out of the pickup, Loper said, "You couldn't load the bull?"

"Of course I loaded the bull. When you send a man to do a man's job, he gets it done."

Loper pointed to the trailer. "Where's the bull?"

Slim looked toward the trailer and saw that it was empty. His eyes grew wide. "Loper, when I left the east pasture pens, that bull was in the trailer. What in the world?"

They walked to the trailer and gave it an inspection. Loper pointed to the trailer gate. "There's your answer. The sliding gate came open and you unloaded a bull somewhere on the county road."

Slim smacked his forehead with the palm of his hand. "Good honk. I never use that sliding gate and I didn't check to see if it was latched."

"I can tell you: it wasn't latched. On that bumpy road, it worked itself open. How fast were you driving?"

"Not fast, twenty or thirty miles an hour."

"Well, if he didn't break a leg, he'll be out on the road somewhere between here and the east pasture."

"We'd better saddle the horses."

Loper shook his head. "I just turned 'em out, and we won't need horses anyway. That bull's as gentle as a pup. We'll take three corral panels and make a wing, and load him afoot."

"I think we ought to take horses."

"It would take too long. I've got a meeting at church at four o'clock and there's only so much time in my schedule to clean up your messes. The next time we need to move a bull, I'll send Alfred to do it."

Slim shook his head and rolled his eyes up to the sky. "Loper, you are the most..."

They were still arguing when they got into the pickup. Loper started the motor and pulled away from the corrals. I didn't do Escort this time because...well, to be real honest, I didn't want to call attention to the fact that they had left me behind.

See, most of the time, a loyal cowdog *wants* to go along on every adventure and, you know, be right there in the middle of things, but when the adventure involves a bull...uh, that changes things. Bulls are huge and they don't like dogs. We don't like them either, so any time we can solve a bull problem without putting the Security Division at risk, we consider it a good deal all the way around.

I had every confidence that they could handle the situation without my help. I mean, two grown men ought to be able to...huh? The pickup slid to a stop and...you know, I had a bad feeling about this, and just in case they had come up with some crazy idea, I tucked my tail and began creeping toward...

"Hank, come here!"

CHAPTER THREE

I Volunteer For a Dangerous Mission

I began creeping toward the hay shed. If you recall, the door of the shed was warped at the bottom and it was no problem for a dog to slip inside.

"Hank!"

I didn't hear anything, did you? Good.

Anyway, as I was saying, it had been weeks since I'd done an inspection of the hay shed and, well, this seemed a good time for me to check things out. You never know what you might find. If the roof has been leaking, the hay can start to mold, and...

"Hank, come here!"

...and who needs moldy hay? Horses won't eat it, so it's very, very important that we monitor the condition of our...huh? Holy smokes, inside

22

the gloomy darkness of the shed, I came face to face with some kind of animal, a carbon-based life form that was staring at me with two eyes. Or was it three?

It spoke. "Oh hi. What are you doing in here?"

I almost fainted with relief when I recognized the voice. "Drover? I thought you were in the machine shed."

"Well, I was, but I saw a black widow spider, so I came here."

"Hank!"

Drover perked one ear. "I think they're calling you."

"They're not calling me. You're mistaken."

"Hank, come here!"

I cut my eyes from side to side. "Okay, they're calling me. The problem is, I don't want to be called."

"Gosh, how come?"

"That's none of your business. Here's the plan. I'm going to hide. If someone comes to the door, tell them I'm not here."

"Yeah, but you are here."

"Drover, sometimes in the line of duty..." Suddenly an idea popped into my head. "Wait. Why don't you go with them?"

"Where are they going?"

23

"Well, that's the good part. They're going to town to buy ice cream cones."

His eyes lit up. "No fooling? Boy, I love ice cream."

"There you go. That will be your reward for being a good little doggie."

"I thought you were mad at me."

"Mad? Me? Ha ha. Where'd you ever get an idea like that?" I heard footsteps approaching. "Well, have a nice trip and enjoy that ice cream. And remember, I'm not here."

"Got it."

I slithered myself behind a bale of prairie hay and pressed my entire body against the floor. In the half-darkness, I became an invisible dog. Pretty clever, huh? You bet, I mean, things had turned out for the best. Drover would get a chance to go for a ride with the boys, and I would get a chance to, uh, catch up on some paperwork.

In the silence, I heard the door hinges squeak, then Slim's voice. "Hello, Stub Tail. Where's Bozo?"

Who? Oh yes, that was one of Slim's names for me: Bozo. I'd never figured out what it meant, but it didn't matter, as long as Drover kept his trap shut.

"Where's Hank? I know he's in here. Oh-h-h,

24

so he's trying to hide, huh? Behind that bale of hay?" The next thing I knew, Slim was towering over me like a telephone pole with a sly grin on his face. "Hi, puppy. We might need your help on a little job."

I lifted my head and began tapping out a message with my tail. It said, "There's no way you could have found me. I'm not here. Go away. I refuse to be bullied into..."

I tried to escape, but he caught me by the tail and swept me up in his arms. In other words, I got shanghaied and pressed into service against my will.

As we were leaving the shed, I glanced around for Drover, hoping to give him a blast of thunder and to call him just what he was: a traitor, a turncoat, a rat, a little squealer, and tattletale. But I didn't get the chance. The little mutter-mumble had vanished like a puff of smoke in a hurricane.

How does he do that?

Slim carried me all the way to the pickup and pitched me into to the cab. That's an important clue. It tells you that they didn't trust me to ride in the back, as though they thought I would jump out.

That's sad, isn't it? What has the world come

to when cowboys can't trust their own dog?

We drove up to the mailbox, turned right on the county road, and headed east. About a mile down the road, we saw the bull: alive, standing on all four legs, and grazing on the tall grass in the ditch. The only evidence of his tumble out of the trailer was a bald spot on his hind end.

Loper stopped the pickup and studied the scene. "Looks like he did a cartwheel, but at least you didn't kill him. I'll try to remember that when I'm figuring your paycheck."

Slim smiled and shook his head. "I'll swan, Loper, your wife must be a saint. I don't know how she's put up with you all these years. What is so hard about admitting that *you* forgot to latch the sliding gate? We've all done it at one time or another. It don't mean that you're a terrible person."

"Are you through?"

"Well, not exactly. I had a couple of more things I wanted to say."

"Too bad. I'll park the pickup against the fence and we'll baling-wire the panels to the left side of the trailer. That'll give us a funnel. We'll walk him down the fence and into the trailer."

Slim nodded. "Sounds like a plan. What about the dog?"

"We'll leave him in the pickup 'til we see how it goes. If my idea doesn't work, we may have to use him for bait."

BAIT! What was that supposed to mean?

Loper parked the pickup and trailer in the south ditch, right next to a five-wire barbed wire fence. They got out of the pickup. I tried to slip out behind Loper, but he slammed the door in my face. Okay, it appeared that they wanted me to stay in the cab.

After they'd set up their wing of panels and opened the trailer gate, they started walking toward the bull. Loper said, "Try not to get him stirred up."

Slim stared at him. "Try not to get him stirred up? Golly gee, what a great idea! You know, my first thought was to chase him around and get him mad, so we could have a little fun."

"Slim, just hush."

They approached the bull in a slow, quiet manner, and got behind him. He was a Hereford bull with big horns. He probably weighed 2,000 pounds and had a neck on him like the trunk of a cottonwood tree. He raised his head and studied the men. He swished his tail and put his head down for another bite of grass.

Loper nodded. "Looking good. Let's ease him

toward the trailer. Go on, bull, we're going to give you a ride home." They moved toward the bull. He turned and started ambling toward the trailer. Loper was looking more relaxed now. "See, when you handle cattle the right way, you don't need horses."

"He ain't loaded yet."

The bull walked straight to the open trailer, and the men followed, keeping pressure on him. The bull sniffed the trailer.

"Go on, bully, step up, and we'll be on our way."

The bull lifted his left front foot and set it down on the trailer floor. It made a hollow sound. The bull removed his foot and turned around, facing the men. He swished his tail and flicked his ears.

Slim said, "He didn't go in. Now what?"

"He's all right. We'll give him a minute to think about it."

The bull thought about it, and at the end of his minute, he snorted, lowered his head, and started pawing up dirt. Loper took a step toward him and waved his hands. "Go on, bull, step up in the..."

I don't think Loper expected the bull to come after him like something that had been shot out of a cannon, but that's what he did, and we're talking about two thousand pounds of meat that was moving on. Loper turned tail and ran towards the pickup, but the bull cut him off, so he headed for the nearest tree, grabbed a limb, and swung out of danger, just as the bull arrived and started butting the trunk.

Slim was standing behind the panel wing and started laughing. The bull heard him, whirled around, and charged. Slim's eyes popped wide open and he made a dash for the pickup, and hopped into the back end just in time. Crunch. The bull bashed the side of the pickup, bellered, shook his head, and glared up at Slim with a pair of flaming eyes.

While this was going on, Loper decided he would climb down out of the tree and...I don't know what he had in mind, but the bull heard him, swapped ends, and made another run at the tree. Loper scrambled back to the limb where he'd been before.

Slim yelled, "Well, I'm sure glad we didn't bring horses."

And Loper yelled back, "Dry up! What did you expect? After you unloaded him at thirty-five miles an hour, he's in a bad mood."

"I think you could say that, yes, but I was only going twenty." For several long minutes, nobody

said a word. Birds chirped and a locust hummed in the distance. Slim broke the silence. "Loper, I hate to ask this, but do you have a Plan B?"

"Turn out the dog. He can't mess things up any worse than they already are."

HUH? Turn out the dog? Hey, unless I was badly mistaken, they were talking about ME! And you know what? That struck me as a real bad idea.

CHAPTER FOUR

This Gets Pretty Scary

Slim crept out of the pickup bed and eased toward the door on the passenger side. The bull heard him, and here he came!

I needed to hide, but where do you hide in the cab of a pickup? I dashed back and forth across the seat and tried to dive out the half-opened window. Gulk. No luck there, so I hit the floorboard on the driver's side and pressed myself against the door.

Maybe Slim wouldn't notice me.

He came flying into the cab and slammed the door behind him, just as the bull arrived, snorting and roaring. Oh, and he started butting the right front tire, which caused the whole pickup to rock back and forth.

Slim mopped the sweat off his forehead and swung his gaze down to me. "Hankie, have you ever dreamed of being a hero?"

No.

"I'm sure you have, so you'll be thrilled to hear this. We need a volunteer."

Forget that.

"The boss is up a tree and I'm trapped in here, and we're about ready to launch Plan B. We think you might be able to help."

Ha.

"Here's the deal. I'm going to chunk you out the window..."

No way, buddy!

"...and we'll see what you can do. We'd be real proud if you could lure the bull into the trailer. Get that done and I'll promise you Double Dog Food."

Oh brother!

"Or just keep the bull busy, so we can get the boss-man out of the tree. You ready?"

Absolutely not! No!

He wasn't kidding. He grabbed me by a hind leg and pulled me out of my hiding place, rolled down the window, and pitched me outside. "Go get 'im, Hankie! This one is for the ranch."

Yeah, right.

The bull was standing about ten feet away from where I landed. He'd been whamming his head against the tire, and when he heard me hit the ground, he turned in my direction.

Those eyes! They sent electrical shivers up and down my spine. I mean, you talk about UGLY! Those were the ugliest, meanest eyes I'd ever seen. I swallowed hard and tried to control the shaking of my legs.

"Hi, Mr. Bull. You're probably wondering what I'm doing here, so let me explain. My employers have asked me to talk to you about... well, about your attitude. Everybody understands that you took a nasty spill this afternoon, but... why are you shaking your horns? Everybody understands...why are you looking at me in that tone of voice? Anyway, we were hoping that..."

Talking to a bull is a tee-total waste of time. You might as well try to reason with a tree. No, bulls are worse than trees, because they hate dogs and will sometimes try to destroy them. That's what this one had in mind when he lowered his head and came after me. I mean, we're talking about a freight train, a serious freight train.

At that point, I did what any normal, healthy American dog would have done. I delivered one stern bark and ran like a striped ape. I don't know how many times we ran back and forth in front of the pickup and trailer. I lost count on three.

Whilst the big galoot was trying to skin me alive, Loper saw his opportunity to climb down out of the tree. Once on the ground, he yelled, "Lead him into the trailer, Hank! The trailer!"

The trailer? Was he joking? Hey, I was just trying to stay alive. But Loper's yelling had one good effect: it alerted the bull that he had another target on the ground, so he went after Loper again. You never saw a cowboy shinny up a tree so fast. I mean, it was pretty funny.

At that point, Slim had worked up enough courage to venture out of the pickup. He found an empty feed sack and started shaking it and making his cattle call: "Woooo, bull, wooo! Come on, bully, come to feed." Sometimes that works, you know. When you can't drive an animal, sometimes you can coax him to come to a feed sack.

The bull came, all right, but not the way Slim had hoped. He came at about twenty-five miles an hour—head down, horns out, brush snapping, and clumps of dirt and grass flying off his hooves. Slim gave him the sack and went flying into the bed of the pickup. I, uh, seized the opportunity to squirt under the trailer.

So there we were: Loper up a tree, Slim in the back of the pickup, and me under the trailer, with the bull storming from one location to another, threatening to stomp the everlasting snot out of the first one that showed himself.

Slim found a shovel in the back of the pickup and whammed the bull between the horns several times. Loper pulled a dead limb off the tree and gave him a few whacks. Me? I barked, of course, and we're talking about deep manly barks.

How much good did it do? Zero. This went on for ten minutes, and with each passing minute, we became more and more aware of the fact that...well, we looked pretty ridiculous. Slim was really disgusted.

He said, "Well, I'm glad *Western Horseman* ain't here to do an article on The Great American Cowboy. This is the most pathetic farmer-looking deal I was ever associated with: two treed cowboys and one dog under the trailer!"

"Well, do something!"

"Do what?"

"I don't know, throw rocks at him! I've got a meeting at four o'clock."

"Moe, Larry, and Curly, where are you?"

At that point, something amazing happened. You won't believe this.

Okay, our ranch crew was in the process of receiving one of the most humiliating defeats in history. We had set out on a simple task, to load a bull, and the bull had ended up loading us.

I was embarrassed. Loper was mad. Slim was beyond mad. But then something really strange happened. A big yellow Labrador retriever stumbled out of some wild plum thickets on the south side of the road, and—this is the most amazing part, so pay attention—on his head he was wearing a BIRD CAGE!

I'm not kidding. A bird cage!

Slim was the first to see it. "Good honk, what IS THAT?"

Loper squinted his eyes and looked. I squinted my eyes and looked. Neither of us could believe what we were seeing. But here's the best part: the bull couldn't believe it either. He had no idea what that thing was that had just stepped out of the brush, but he'd never seen one before and he wanted no part of it.

He jerked his head back and forth, swished his tail, darted to the left, ran straight to the trailer door, and hopped inside. I'm not joking. I saw it with my own eyes. The bull loaded himself!

For several long seconds, we all stared and blinked back our astonishment. Then Loper yelled, "Don't just sit there, shut the gate!"

Slim sprang out of the back of the pickup, rushed to the trailer, and closed the gate. His hands were shaking so badly, it took him fifteen seconds to secure the latch. If the bull had whirled around and hit the gate, old Slim would have been wearing it for a necktie.

But you know what? That bull—the same big oaf that had terrorized two cowboys and one top-of-the-line cowdog for thirty minutes—that one-ton hunk of pure meanness stood there like a lamb and didn't move a hair.

Once Slim had gotten the gate latched, he almost fainted with relief. Loper climbed down from the tree and tried to put on a dignified face. Me? I rushed out from under the trailer and delivered a withering barrage of barking.

The three of us met at the rear of the trailer, and at that point, we turned our gazes upon the guy who had loaded our bull, the yellow Lab. There he stood, grinning at us and swinging his long, thick tail back and forth. He looked about as smart as a cord of wood.

Loper was the first to speak. "Nobody's going to believe this story."

Slim shook his head. "Where in the cat hair would a dog find a bird cage out here?"

"I have no idea. What'll we do with him? He's not wearing a collar."

Slim mopped his face on the sleeve of his shirt. "Well, I'd say take him to the house and give him a good feed. He deserves it. He sure bailed you out of a mess."

Loper grumbled something under his breath, went to the dog, and pried the bird cage off his head. It wasn't so easy. The mutt had stuck his big head through a little door that had been built for canaries. Loper gave him a pat on the head and pointed toward the back of the pickup. "Load up. Jump."

The big lug grinned and thrashed his tail. Apparently he didn't understand "load up" or "jump," so Slim had to pick him up (with much grunting and wheezing, I mean, that was a big dog) and pitch him in the back. I had planned on riding up front with the executives, but Loper's mood had soured and he made me ride in the back.

Okay, fine. If they didn't want my company...I leaped into the back and we headed for home. Up in the cab, the argument raged on.

Slim growled, "It sure makes me proud,

working on a real cowboy outfit."

"Oh, dry up, will you? If you're such a hot-rod cowboy, how come you unloaded my bull in the middle of the county road?"

"Well, for the simple reason that the owner of this outfit forgot to latch the sliding gate."

"And the head-cowboy never checks his equipment."

"Are you ever going to admit that you caused this whole mess?"

"No, but I might dock your paycheck for putting skid marks on the livestock."

"Loper, you are the stubbornest, hard-headedest, mule-temperedest man I ever met."

On and on. Those two could argue for days about nothing. Tomorrow, they would pick another topic and argue about that.

I rode back to headquarters with Bird Cage. He faced the front and seemed to be perfectly content, letting the wind blow across his big floppy tongue. I didn't try to make conversation. To be honest, I really didn't care about the details of his life. He had stumbled into my world without being invited, and until we sent him down the road, he was going to be nothing but a problem.

Does that sound harsh and unfriendly? Maybe

so, but I don't care. Hey, this isn't a dude ranch or a resort for lost dogs. We have work to do, and no time to entertain visitors.

Back at headquarters, we unloaded the bull in the corrals. He circled the front pen a couple of times, and stopped when he saw me sitting on the other side of the board fence. Down went his head and he started pawing up dirt again—the same silly routine we'd seen before.

As you might expect, I conducted myself as a mature gentleman. "Hey, jerk, do you think anyone around here is scared of you? Ha. You're pathetic. If you're so tough, how come we got you loaded in the trailer, huh? It was like loading sheep, easiest job I ever had. Oh, and that business about you taking a spill on the county road? Very shrewd, pal. You need to try that again sometime."

Hee hee. I love tormenting bulls, and the more dirt they paw up, the better I like it. Of course, it helps to have a good stout fence between us.

CHAPTER FIVE

The Bird-Cage Dog

Slim and Loper drifted down to the house and found Sally May, Alfred, and Baby Molly out in the yard. Loper told them about our big adventure and introduced them to Bird Cage. Sally May came out the gate and stroked him on the head.

"He's a sweet dog...but what will you do with him?"

Loper shrugged. "I guess we'll just keep him around until we can find the owners. Somebody will be looking for him. They'll show up."

"Look at the size of his feet! Well, what should we call him?

Slim was slouching against the gate post. "How about Blunderbuss? He ain't too graceful."

Sally May shot him a glare. "Blunderbuss! What an awful name for a nice dog." She looked down at the mutt and smiled. "He has such a happy face. How about Happy?"

Loper nodded. "Works for me. Let's get him some groceries. I 'spect he hasn't had much to eat for the past few days."

Sally May laughed. "I imagine not—wearing a bird cage on his head."

Sally May and the baby stayed at the house, and the rest of us escorted Happy Bird Cage up to the machine shed. Slim fetched a fifty-pound sack of dog food and filled the overturned Ford hubcap that served as our dog bowl.

Have you ever been around while a Labrador was eating? To put it in polite language, they are "eager eaters." I mean, this guy went through a bowl of Co-op like it was a snack for ants: slurp, slop, gone. And whilst he was wolfing it down, his tail was swinging around like a tree limb in a high wind. I know, because it caught me on the left side of the jaw and almost knocked me out.

"Hey, goofball, watch the tail!"

He didn't even notice. By then, he was licking the crumbs off the bottom of the bowl and begging for more. Slim filled the bowl again and the big oaf went through it in about two minutes, and was ready for thirds. He didn't get thirds. By that time, Loper had begun to wonder if the ranch could afford the luxury of having a lost Lab on the place.

We walked down to the gas tanks and Loper pointed to the gunny sacks. "Happy, this is the bunkhouse. Stay out of the yard, leave the cat alone, and don't bark in the night, and we'll get along fine." He turned to me. "Hank, show him the ropes and keep him in line."

Me? Keep him in line? Hey, I hadn't invited him. I hardly knew the guy and I hadn't been hired to be a babysitter for stray dogs.

Loper bent at the waist and brought his face close to mine. "By the way, the next time I need help loading a bull, I'll drive to town and rent a poodle."

I stared into his eyes. I couldn't believe he'd said that. *Rent a poodle*! I'd never been so insulted. What a low-down cheap shot! For his information...

He didn't wait around to hear my defense. He never does. As I've said before, these people really don't want to know what their dogs think. But this is still America, by George, and for the record, here's what I thought about his outrageous comment.

People who talk about renting poodles don't know beans about dogs. If they did, they'd show more respect for the cowdog breeds. Not only do we have keen instincts about livestock...okay, maybe my performance hadn't been so great, but what about Loper's performance? We're talking about a grown man, a self-described "cattleman," who'd spent part of his afternoon hiding in a tree!

I wished we'd made a movie of the entire episode. I would have run it forwards and backwards. An audience of normal people would have laughed themselves silly. I mean, how many times did the bull put him up the tree? Twice? Three times? What kind of example was he setting for his dogs? Hey, when the boss-man climbs a tree, what do they expect the dogs to do—march off to battle and get creamed?

Rent a poodle! What an insult.

Where were we? I got so caught up defending my reputation...oh yes, Loper didn't hang around to hear my side of things. He had some big meeting at the church, remember? I wish I could have attended that meeting. I would have told his church friends all about the clown job I had witnessed that very...

Oh well, a dog can't allow himself to dwell on Life's injustice. There are some things we can control and other things that we can only grumble about.

The point is that Loper left the ranch and drove into town, and Slim started mowing grass, which left me alone with Happy Bird Cage. There we were, just the two of us in the Security Division's Vast Office Complex, me and a seventy-five pound, loose-hided, floppy eared, town-raised dingbat Labrador who had been dropped in my lap. He was even sitting on my gunny sack bed!

"Okay, pal, let's get this over with. I'm Hank the Cowdog, Head of Ranch Security. You'll be taking orders from me."

He gave me his happy grin. "Hi."

"Number One, you see that gunny sack you're sitting on? That's *mine*. Never sit or lie on my gunny sack. Do you copy?"

"You mean..."

"Move! On this ranch, we don't say please. We don't draw pictures or furnish Crayons. Stay off my gunny sack."

"Gee whiz, I didn't know..."

"Nobody cares what you don't know. If we did, we'd die of a broken heart, because what you don't know is *everything*."

"So...you'd like for me to move, right?" Before I could scream in his face, he moved over to

Drover's gunny sack. "Is this better?"

"It's better. It's not best."

"I always try to do my best."

"Listen, genius, I'm not cruel enough to tell you what would be best for me, for you, for the whole ranch, so let's move along. Number Two, they've dumped you on the Security Division and there's nothing I can do about that. You should understand that you're the new guy, a rookie, and we don't like rookies. Don't do anything that makes the rest of us look bad. Do you copy?"

"Oh, I'd never do that."

"You already did. You loaded a bull that the rest of us couldn't load."

"What bull? Oh, you mean that cow that hopped into the trailer?"

"That wasn't a cow, it was a fighting bull. Through incredible dumb luck, you managed to scare him into the trailer, and now everybody thinks you're some kind of hero. That makes me look bad, understand?"

"Not really. What should I have done?"

The question caught me off guard. "I don't know, but whatever you did, you shouldn't have done, and whatever you should have done, you didn't do. Am I making myself clear?" He gave me a blank stare. "Never mind. Where in thunderation did you find a bird cage?"

He scowled. "I'm not certain about that. See, I've been as lost as a goose for two days and..." He glanced all around. "You know, this is a big place out here."

"Answer the question. Where did you find the bird cage?"

"Well sir, I was walking around and I seen it in a pile of junk."

"Okay, next question. Why would a dog stick his head into a bird cage?"

His smile slipped a little. "Boy, that's a good one. It's a natural question to ask, isn't it?"

"Yes. Some of us would say that it wasn't the smartest thing you ever did."

"Yes sir, that's kind of what I thought...after I done it. I mean, that little bitty door didn't hardly fit my neck."

"So why did you do it?"

He gave that a moment's thought. "It kind of snuck up on me. I smelt a bird and seen a hole, and next thing I knew, I was wearing the darned cage."

"You smelled a bird?" I narrowed my eyes and gave him a careful looking-over. "Labrador *retriever*. You're a bird dog, right?"

"Supposed to be, but my nose isn't too good."

"You're a bird dog and that explains everything. Oh brother! Once again, I'm stuck with a Birdly Wonder." I paced a few steps away from him and tried to calm my nerves. "What are you doing out here? Don't you have a home?"

He had to think about that for a moment. "Yes, I have a home and a family, or used to."

"So where are they? What happened?"

"That's a little hazy. We were having a picnic and I think I wandered off, and this pickup came down the road and stopped." He gazed off into the distance and smiled. "The driver told me to hop in and I hopped in and we drove some more and he let me out, and I've been lost ever since. Does that make sense?"

"No. Why would you jump into a stranger's pickup?"

"Well, he was a nice feller, and...I don't know, it just seemed like a good idea at the time. Maybe it wasn't all that great."

"It wasn't a great idea, take my word for it. You walked away from a good home, and now you're lost—which, by the way, is typical bird dog behavior."

He glanced around and licked his chops. "Say, what time do y'all eat around here? I'm starved."

I paced over to him and gave him a snarl. "I'm

glad you brought that up. You've already eaten. I was there and watched. You ate like five pigs!"

"Well, I'm a big guy and I get hungry."

"Too bad. You eat too much. This ranch can't afford your appetite."

He heaved a sigh. "I think I'm getting off to a bad start."

"Exactly right. Let's try not to make it even worse. Now, if you'll excuse me, I've got work to do."

"Maybe I can help."

"No. You can't help. I don't need a bird dog tagging along behind me. Stay here and try not to mess anything up."

"I hope I'm not a burden."

"You *are* a burden, but I guess you can't help it. Stay off my gunny sack."

"Yes sir." He stretched out on Drover's gunny sack and lay still, with his eyes open. To be honest, he looked kind of...okay, maybe he looked sad. Was that my fault? No, it wasn't my fault, and I refused to worry about it.

In my line of work, a guy can't allow himself to get weepy and sentimental about every little thing that happens. See, my ranch is the Real World, not some smoochy love story where dogs grin all the time and nobody ever gets crabby.

You might recall that I live around people who gripe at me all the time. Remember Loper's latest insult? "Next time I need help loading a bull, I'll go to town and rent a poodle."

You think that didn't run a spear right through my heart? Cowdogs have pride, and that hurt, but you won't catch me sniffling and whining about it. No sir, I take my lumps and go back to work. If Happy Bird Cage had gotten his feelings hurt, that was too bad. He needed to develop a few calluses.

The point is that I didn't have time to worry about hurting the feelings of a stray bird dog, but the even larger point is that...well, as I was making my evening patrol of ranch headquarters, I found myself...uh...thinking that maybe I'd been too hard on the big lug.

This was his first day on the place, after all, and he seemed to be a pretty decent sort of fellow. In spite of myself, I kind of liked his big happy grin, and when I'd seen him lying there with sadness in his eyes...

Oh brother. I canceled my Evening Walk-Around of headquarters and returned to the office.

CHAPTER SIX

Happy Lab

When I saw the empty gunny sack, a wave of concern swept over me. Happy was gone. My eyes darted around and my mind swirled. What had I done?

At that moment, my ears picked up odd sounds that seemed to be coming from a location to the east. I lifted Earoscanners and zeroed in on the sounds. Moments later, I got a reading from Data Control: "Lawn mower and a child's laughter, probably coming from the yard."

I hurried away from the office and followed the sounds. Approximately seventy-five feet from the yard gate, I stopped and took a visual reading, and saw an amazing sight. Slim Chance was driving the riding lawn mower around the gravel drive, and beside him on the seat was seventy-five pounds of grinning bird dog. Happy Lab was riding on the lawn mower, if you can believe that, and everyone loved it. Even Sally May was laughing.

After a while, Slim stopped the mower and Happy stepped down. Little Alfred led him into the yard, climbed on his back, and started riding him like a horse, using Hap's big ears for bridle reins. The kid was having the time of his life, and so was the dog. Hap staggered under the weight of his load but never lost that big sloppy grin, with his tongue hanging out the side of his mouth. When Alfred lost his balance and fell off, Hap licked him on the cheek and waited for him to remount, and off they went again.

It was really something to see, and though I didn't particularly want to be impressed, I was. If you'd wanted to capture the scene with a song, it would have gone something like this.

Happy Dog

Happy day, happy night,
Happy eating appetite.
Wag your tail, run and hide,
Give the kids a pony ride.

Happy dog, pollywog,
Fetch a stick, chase a frog.
Eat your food, don't be rude.
Always smile.

Deedle dee, deedle dum.
Fiddle faddle fodle fum.
Rickie tick, rockie tock.
Snicker doodle bobbie socks.

Dingaling, birdies sing
Tickle tockle tammerling.
Murgle skiffer rambling.
Always smile.

I watched for several minutes and returned to the office. For some reason, it left me feeling... well, depressed.

Half an hour later, when Sally May called Alfred into the house for supper, I heard big footsteps approaching. Happy chugged into the office, said "Hi," and flopped down on Drover's bed. He stretched out and appeared to be ready for sleep.

I broke the silence. "You're good with kids."

He sat up and looked at me. "Beg pardon?"

"I said, you're good with kids."

"Oh, thanks. Yeah, I like 'em."

"I like 'em too, but only up to a point. I can't believe how patient you were with Alfred, letting him ride you around. Doesn't that hurt your back?"

"Oh yes, a little. Mostly it bothers my hips."

"So...why did you do it? I mean, most dogs wouldn't stand for it."

He gazed up at the sky and took a deep breath. "A guy likes to do what he's good at. Maybe it makes up for all the things he don't do so well."

"Explain that."

His eyes drifted down to me. "I'm not a very good bird dog—near-sighted, can't smell, can't find a covey of birds, can't retrieve. And when they start shooting off guns...I'm scared of loud noises. Guns go off, I'm out of there."

"Hmmm. That's not so good—I mean, for a bird dog."

"Yeah, but it's worse than that. I do things that are ridiculous, all the time."

"Ridiculous?"

"Yeah, like sticking my head into a bird cage. That was really a dumb thing to do."

I laughed. "I can't argue with that."

"I do stuff like that. I chew things up and dig holes and knock over flower pots. Listen, buddy,

58

I ate a garden hose one time—three feet of rubber hose."

"You swallowed it?"

"I did. I was sick for three days."

I didn't want to laugh but, well, that was pretty funny. "That's a hard way to learn, but I bet you didn't try it again." There was a long moment of silence. "You didn't try it again, did you?" Another silence. "You did?"

"That's what I'm telling you. I do ridiculous things, over and over. I really didn't want you to know all this."

I got up and paced a few steps away. The sun had dropped below the horizon and pleasant smells hung in the air. "Okay, Hap, let's talk. First of all, I'm sorry I've been so grouchy. I'm ashamed of myself. Second, it appears that you're going to be here on the ranch for a while, and third, while you're here, you must refrain from doing ridiculous things."

"Yeah, I've been worrying about that. I just don't know how to act."

I whirled around and paced back to him. "It's very simple. When you get an urge to do something ridiculous, *don't do it*. Say no to the urge."

"Sounds good, but it don't always work."

"All right, then here's an idea." I laid a paw on his big shoulder. "When you get a silly notion, find me and we'll talk it out. I'm willing to help if you're willing to let me."

"No kidding?"

"Absolutely. Look, we dogs are in this together. You helped us load a bad bull, maybe I can help you resist crazy ideas. What do you think?"

His eyes filled with tears. "Nobody's ever cared that much about me. I just hope you won't be disappointed."

My eyes grew misty and I turned away. In a voice that trembled with emotion, I said, "Happy, with two sincere, intelligent dogs working on this deal, what could go wrong?"

That was a pretty emotional scene, wasn't it? You bet. And to be honest, it left me a little dizzy. I mean, I'd started the afternoon mad at him, just because he was there, and ended up talking to him as though we were old friends.

It doesn't make much sense unless you factor this into the equation: it's hard to stay mad at a Lab. They are such nice, happy, honest, decent guys, who can *not* like them? Any time I get to thinking that I'm a good dog, all I have to do is hang out with the nearest Lab for an hour and that sets the record straight.

I'm *not* a lab, not even close. Labs seem to be born nice and kind and gentle and everything else a dog should be, and it comes without effort.

Yes, I know they're bird dogs and, yes, I don't like bird dogs (Plato comes to mind), but...it's confusing, isn't it? Just when you think you've got Life figured out, a Lab shows up at the ranch and blows all your theories.

So there we were in my bedroom/office under the gas tanks. I curled up on my gunny sack and Happy sprawled out on Drover's. Perhaps you're wondering what had become of Drover, and here's the scoop on that.

Around sundown, he came skipping down the hill, stopped in his tracks, took one look at the big lug that was occupying his bed, did a one-eighty, and left. I saw him and yelled, "Hey, where are you going?"

"It's too crowded. I'm leaving."

That was it. He trotted back to the machine shed and disappeared inside. Make no mistake, that's a weird little mutt.

Oh well. Hap and I had our bunks and we put them to good use. Within moments, Hap was conked out and doing some serious snoring. Over the years, I had adjusted to Drover's sleeping patterns, which included a whole orchestra of mostly-comical sounds: squeaks, wheezes, whistles, honks, grunts, and periods of incoherent babbling.

Hap's night-noise was something different. Big dogs make big noise, and we're talking about a soundtrack that included trucks, trains, bulldozers, motor-graders, elephants, and water buffalo. As a snorer, he belonged in the same class with Slim Chance, who could bend rafters and burst water lines.

I thought I would never get to sleep, but did, finally, and didn't even crack an eye until something woke me up in the middle of the night. I heard my name. "Hank? I think you'd better wake up."

My eyes flew open and I leaped to my...let's be honest here. I *sloshed* to my feet, and although my eyes might have been open, they weren't seeing much that made sense. I saw this...this water buffalo standing in front of me, only he was a blondish-yellow color instead of brown.

In my confusion, I blurted out, "You're supposed to be plowing the rice paddy, and two pounds of garlic will never make a sandwich." I blinked my eyes and glanced around. "Where am I? Who are you?"

"It's me, Happy. I'm sorry to bother you."

"No, that's okay, I was awake and watching the construction."

"What construction?"

"They're building a new highway. I heard trucks and bulldozers."

"Where?"

"Right over there. No, wait, it was a rice paddy. They were using water buffalo to...who did you say you were?"

"Happy, the new guy, Labrador. Remember?"

"Oh yes, of course." I took a few steps and tried to clear my head. "Okay, I'll take charge. We need to get those water buffalo out of here. They're very destructive. If they get into Sally May's yard..." I paced back over to him. "Did you see any water buffalo?"

"Nope. Well, maybe. I spotted something in the yard. I was going to bark at it, but figured I'd better check with you first."

"Good thinking. Barking at night can get a dog into big trouble on this outfit."

He rolled his eyes around. "Maybe you could come with me and check it out. I don't want to do anything foolish."

"Right. I remember now. We want to prevent Ridiculous Behavior at all costs."

"Boy, yeah, especially my first night here."

"Exactly. I'm glad you called. Let's go check it out."

We crept through the darkness and made our way toward the house. I took the Lead Position because...well, because that's what I do. Some dogs are born to lead and some are born to swallow. Follow.

About halfway there, I broke the silence. "Let's go over this again. How did this get started? I need facts, details."

"Well, sir, what woke me up was...well, I get hungry in the night."

"Hap, I stood there and watched you gulp down two bowls of Co-op dog food."

"I know, but I get hungry. Wait, we'd better stop here." We stopped and he pointed his paw to the east. "Lookie yonder and tell me what that is."

I switched my eyes over to Infra-freckle Night Vision and scanned the yard. "What I see is the lawn mower."

"Well, that's what I thought too, at first, but then...it moved."

"It moved?"

"Yes sir, it moved. I think it moved. Yes."

I took a closer look. "That's the riding lawn mower. Slim must have left it in the yard. See the handle bars?"

"Well, I thought that too, but I kept looking and...I think those are horns."

"Horns?"

"Yes sir. Remember that big cow that hopped in the trailer?"

"He was a bull and...hmmm, he had horns, didn't he?" I adjust the focus on the scanner and zoomed in on the object. "You know what? Those might be horns." I put the scanner away and turned to my comrade. "It's the bull!"

A Bull In
Sally May's Yard

I lowered my voice and spoke to Happy Lab. "How did the bull get out of the corral? Wait. You know those bulldozers and water buffalo I was hearing? It was him, snorting and tearing down the corral fence."

"Well sir, I sure thought something was wrong, but I didn't want to do anything foolish."

I laid a paw on his shoulder. "Hap, there's nothing foolish about reporting a bull in the yard. You did the right thing."

He heaved a big sigh. "Boy, that makes me feel better."

My mind was racing. "We've got a big problem here. The first time we went into combat with this guy, we got skunked, but then you showed up with that bird cage on your head. That spooked him."

"Reckon we ought to look for another bird cage?"

I had to chuckle at that. "There are no bird cages on this ranch. You found the only one in the whole county."

"Gosh, what'll we do?"

"That's the question, isn't it?" I began pacing, as I often do when I'm gazing down at the Chessboard of Life and trying to formaldehyde a plan of battle. "If we went over the fence and stormed the yard, he would clean our clocks."

"Maybe we ought to bark, reckon?"

I paced over to him. "Hap, I'm in charge here. Don't strain yourself." I began pacing again. "We must alert the house and, unfortunately, that means barking. That will expose us to danger on two fronts. Number one, the bull might tear down the fence and come after us. Number two, we could face an enraged Loper or Sally May."

"Who?"

"The people in the house. They don't always understand the deeper layers of meaning when we bark at night."

"Huh. You mean…"

"I mean they get really crabby when we wake

them up, and, we're talking about hostile and irrational, hissing and screeching and hurling threats and insults."

His eyes grew wide. "Wow. Maybe we ought to let it slide."

"I'm afraid it's too late for that. What if the bull is still there in the morning? What if Little Alfred walks out of the house?"

He nodded his big head. "I hear you. We've got to protect the kids."

"Exactly. Hap, a lot of dogs wouldn't care, but you and I...we're different. We have a special place in our hearts for the little children."

A quiver came into his voice. "Yes sir, I get all teary-eyed just thinking about 'em."

"Save it for later. There's a time for tears and there's a time to bark. This is the time to bark, and I mean bark as we've never barked in our whole lives."

He pulled himself up to full-attention. "I'm ready, let's do it."

It was a touching moment, the two of us out there on the field of battle, moments before launching ourselves into combat. But we didn't have time to think about it. We had a job to do.

I gave the signal and we crept forward. About ten feet from the yard gate, I gave the signal to halt, and it was then that I noticed...the cat. He was sitting beside the yard gate, staring at us with his weird cattish eyes.

"Well, well! It's Hankie the Wonderdog, with a friend."

"Pete, we're on a mission and I don't have time for chatter. Hap and I are here to do something about that bull."

"Oh really. What bull?"

"There's a bull in the yard, right over there."

Pete twisted his head all around and searched the yard. Then his eyes popped open. "Oh, that bull!"

"Stand back and try to stay out of the way. We're fixing to unload some heavy ordinance."

"Oh good, good! I'll take cover."

"You do that. Or don't, I don't care." The cat disappeared into the shadows and I turned to my comrade. "The bull hasn't moved. It makes me wonder..."

"Oh, he moved."

"He did? Are you sure?"

"Yes sir, I'm sure. I'm pretty sure. He moved. I think I seen him move."

I studied Happy's face in the pale moonlight and a thought popped into my head. This was the same guy who had confessed that he was prone to

doing ridiculous things. Was there any chance...
nah, surely not.

I took a deep breath. "Okay, this is the Big
Show, what we've been training for all our lives.
You stand over there and I'll set up over here.
Take a wide, comfortable stance. On my signal,
we'll cut loose with Number Three Artillery
Barks."

"What's that?"

"Your biggest barks, Hap, and don't hold
anything back. If the bull comes after us, it's
every dog for himself. Run for your life."

"Yes sir, got it. I'm locked and livered."

"What did you say?"

"I said, I'm licked and livered."

"It's *locked and loaded*, Hap. Get it right."

"Okay, got it. I'm ready." He gave me a wink.
"You ever hear a Lab bark at night?"

"Not that I can remember, no."

He puffed himself up. "Wait till you hear this.
After dark, nobody out-barks a Lab."

"Good, but wait for my signal."

Happy Lab turned toward the house and
started blasting away. In other words, he didn't
wait for my signal. I thought about scolding him,
but...well, I didn't get the chance.

Remember that thick, heavy tail we discussed

before? Apparently, when Labs do their serious barking, they swing their tail back and forth. Maybe it has something to do with maintaining their balance, I don't know, but when that tail starts swinging, you need to back away and give it some room.

The point is that I got whacked right on the jaw, and it did produce a spray of colored stars and checkers. "Hey, you big ape, watch what you're doing!" He didn't hear me, and by that time, there was no calling him back. He'd gotten into a rhythm and he was firing off a round of barking every four or five seconds.

By then, it was clear that he hadn't been exaggerating about his barking skills. The guy was awesome, and I say that as a dog who's pretty impressed with his own barking ability. He had mastered every detail of the Heavy Barking Procedure: the stance (good, wide, comfortable stance), proper balance (the tail action), breathing technique (big gulps of air), rhythm (one bark after another, no breaks or pauses), and voicing (deep, piercing barks).

Wow, I was blown away. I didn't know whether I was looking at incredible natural talent, or if he had spent years learning his craft, but the result was something close to Art. And there I was, sitting on the front row and watching the whole show.

It was a humbling experience. To be honest, I don't necessarily enjoy feeling humble, but in the presence of Happy Lab, all I could do was watch and gasp and marvel at this amazing display of talent and discipline.

When I finally dared to add my own barks to the effort, I did it with the understanding that, no matter how many hours I practiced, I would never be in the same league with this dog.

But I tried. That's all a dog can do. I mean, life doesn't end when you find out that you're the second-best barking dog in Texas.

So we barked. Oh, did we bark! The moon rattled. The trees quivered. The house trembled. On and on we barked, fighting fatigue and cotton-mouth and legs that were weakened by the relentless recoil of our barks.

At last, we got some results. Inside the house, we heard a voice. "Hank! Knock it off!"

I turned to Happy and managed to gasp, "It's working. Keep cranking 'em out!"

He grinned and yelled, "I'm on it, bud! I love this!"

We kept cranking them out, bark after bark, blast after blast, roar upon roar. We heard another angry scream coming from inside the house. "Idiots! Shut up that barking!"

You know, a guy hates to push his people to the point where they're sitting up in bed and screaming, but what's the alternative? I mean, the whole point of the procedure was to wake 'em up and get 'em out of the house so they could see the danger that was lurking in their yard.

We just do our jobs, even if it isn't always pleasant.

Loper must have been glued into his bed, or maybe he thought that screaming at us from the bedroom would get him off the hook. Nope. We kept pumping out the barks, until at last a light came on in the bedroom, then another light in the kitchen.

I turned to Hap. "He's coming. Keep truckin'."

He paused to grab a breath of air. "Boy, he's a hard-head."

"He is, but he'll be proud of us."

The porch light came on, then the door opened...WHACK...hitting the side of the house, and out he came, like...I don't know, like hissing lava pouring out of a volcano, I suppose.

Gack, you talk about an ugly face! Wrinkles, puffy eyes, smoldering glare, flared nostrils, and hair going every-which way. The man was seriously torqued. The sight of him would have scared a lot of dogs—hey, it scared me and I was his friend—but Hap, bless him, hung right in there, and even dared to edge closer to the bull. He never missed a bark. I had never seen such endurance. The guy was a barking machine.

Loper stomped down the porch steps. At that point, we got our first glimpse at his "outfit," so to speak: boxer shorts, cowboy boots, and nakedness from the waist up. I also picked up a tiny detail that a lot of dogs would have missed: his boots were on the wrong feet. Clearly, he didn't function well at three o'clock in the morning.

He stormed down the sidewalk and came to the fence. His flaming red blood-shot spider-webbed eyes scorched me, then turned to Hap, who was still pumping out barks at the bull.

"Shut up!" We stopped barking and stood at attention. "That," he flung out a finger at the bull, "is a LAWN MOWER!"

Hap and I shifted our eyes in the direction of his finger and took another look at the, uh, bull.

"Quit barking at the lawn mower!"

By George, it did appear to be a, uh, lawn mower, a riding lawn mower with handle bars. I turned my gaze around to the bird dog, just in time to see him grin, duck his head, and start

thrashing his tree-limb tail from side to side. Oh, and I heard him say, "Oops."

Loper wasn't finished. "Now listen, you clambrains, I keep a twelve-gauge automatic shotgun beside the back door. It's got one round of number seven birdshot in the barrel and two rounds in the magazine. If I have to come out here again, whichever one of you fools is still barking will be wearing buckshot. Am I making myself clear, Hank?"

Huh? Me? Hey, I wasn't the one who'd thought it was a bull.

His glare swung around and stabbed the Lab. "And you, Bird Cage, do you hear what I'm saying?"

Happy went into spasms of guilt. He grinned, fawned, ducked his head, moved his front feet up and down, wagged his tree limb, and dribbled down both hind legs. Nobody does Guilt better than a Lab, and you know, I think the guy was totally sincere about it. He really felt bad.

Back to Loper. He placed his arms on the top of the fence and leaned down toward me. "Not one more sound, you meatheads, not even a squeak!"

Yes sir.

He stormed back into the house and slammed the door behind him. BAM!

CHAPTER EIGHT

Who Can Stay
Mad At a Lab?

Whew! Well, Loper had vented his gizzard and it was time for me to vent mine. I stomped over to the bird-brain and pointed to the lawn mower. "It moved, huh?"

"I thought it moved."

"It had horns, huh?"

"They looked like horns."

"Those are handle bars. They're turned the wrong direction to be horns."

"My eyes aren't so good."

"I told you it was a riding lawn mower."

"I see that now. Hank, I feel awful about this. I mean it, I really do." He started...oh brother... he started crying.

"Stop blubbering! It makes you look ridiculous."

He kept blubbering. "What did I tell you? I

keep doing ridiculous things."

"Yes, and remember the advice I gave you? If you'll stop doing ridiculous things, you can stop apologizing for them."

He shook his head. "It doesn't work, nothing helps. I'm just a failure as a dog!"

He bawled and blubbered for...I don't know, three years, it seemed, but maybe it was only two minutes. I had to sit there and listen, and with each passing second, I could feel the pressure of my anger leaking out into the atmosphere.

Like I said, who can stay mad at a Lab? Nobody.

At last I spoke. "You're not a failure and you can't give up hope."

He looked at me through tear-blurred eyes. "How come?"

"Because I said so. This is my ranch and I won't allow it."

"Yeah, but..."

"If you'll quit blubbering, I'll keep working with you. Together, maybe we can whip this thing, but you have to listen to what I tell you."

He brushed a big paw across his face, and that big, wonderful Labrador smile returned. "I'm willing to try, if you are."

"All right, let's start simple." I jabbed him in

the chest with my paw. "You've got bad eyes, so don't bark at anything after dark. If you see something suspicious, call me."

"Yes sir."

"Because if you continue barking at lawn mowers and pickups and roping dummies and trees, you'll get us both fired. We will get canned. They will send us down the road without dog food."

He licked his chops and glanced around. "Boy, I could use a snack."

"You can't have a snack! This is a ranch, not a hotel, and dogs don't get snacks in the middle of the night. Come on, we're returning to barracks, and you *will* go to sleep."

"Yes sir."

I hated to be so hard on him, but if I'm not firm with the men, who will be? They send me misfits and mutton-headed bird dogs, and I'm supposed to make soldiers out of them. Discipline, that's the heart and soul of every fighting unit. When you lose discipline, you're on a sloppery slip.

A slippery slop.

What is the term I'm searching for? You're on a slobbering slick.

Never mind. I hate it when this happens.

You're on slickering slob.

You're on a skippering stick.

Phooey. I can't waste my time chasing words around. It's a common expression and it was right on the slop of my slick.

I get SO ANNOYED when this happens. I mean, you're right in the middle of making a very important point and all you need is one or two words to finish...

When your outfit loses discipline, you're on slippery snick.

That's not it. You know what? I no longer care. Five minutes ago, I cared. I wanted to speak a sentence that was more than mindless rubbish, but I tried and...

Who's causing this? Someone is doing this to us. They're hacking into our systems and planting Mind Maggots, and would you like to guess who is my primary suspect?

The cat. Pete. I have no idea how he does it, but don't forget that he is the Sneak Above All Sneaks. And don't forget that he played a role in the Bull Debacle. Remember that? I asked if he'd seen a bull and he said...

Never mind the cat. He makes me ill.

Where were we? I'm totally lost. Wait, here we go. I had gone out on a mission with Happy

Lab, remember? And it had turned into a disaster, an embarrassment for the entire Security Division. Loper had come out of the house in his underwear and screeched at us. Now, we were returning to barracks.

And the term I was searching for was "slippery slope." When an outfit loses discipline, it's on a slippery slope.

Now we're cooking.

Anyway, on our way back to our bunks, we passed the garden. Happy noticed that the gate was open. (Little Alfred left it open, remember?) And he said, "What's that?"

"Depending on what you're looking at, it's either the garden or the gate into the garden."

He stopped. "Garden. Isn't that where they grow food?"

I heaved a sigh. "Yes, Happy, that's where they grow food, but it's stuff that dogs don't eat. You wouldn't like it, trust me."

"Oh, I wouldn't be so sure about that. I've ate turnips before."

"You're kidding."

"And apples and watermelon."

"You're kidding!"

"No sir. Like I told you, I get hungry. When a big dog gets to craving a snack, he'll eat 'most anything." His eyes were shining. "Would you mind if I checked it out?"

"That's Sally May's territory and she has strict rules. She doesn't allow dogs in the garden."

He gave me a wink. "Yeah, but the gate's open."

"Hap, you have huge feet. Huge feet leave huge tracks."

"Listen, bud, I'm about to starve."

I paced back and forth, trying to gripple with this latest grapple. If Big Boy didn't get a snack, I might be up all night listening to him moan about it. I needed some sleep. I had a ranch to run.

"Okay, we'll work a compromise. There's a compost pit in there. You can have anything in the compost, but leave the garden alone."

"What's compost?"

"It's snack food for dogs that think about eating twenty-four hours a day."

"Hey, that's me. This'll work."

As he lumbered through the gate, I yelled, "Stay away from the plants and watch where you're stepping!"

"Yes sir, got it."

It took him about five seconds to find the compost heap. He had told me that his nose didn't work well on game birds, but he didn't need high-tech equipment to find a compost heap. It was full of rotting and half-rotting vegetable matter, and it stinked. Stank. Even Drover could have found it.

I waited outside the garden, pacing and fuming over this ridiculous waste of time. Soon, I heard him crunching on something. "What are you eating?"

"Hey, I hit the jackpot! Watermelon rinds."

"Watermelon rinds!" I hadn't planned on entering the garden, but I had to see this. When I got there, I found him crunching on a watermelon hull, wearing a huge grin, and looking as content as a hog in a mud hole. "Unbelievable."

"Hey, they crunch kind of like bones. You want to try one?"

"Absolutely not."

"And lookie here." He pointed into the hole.

I peered into the compost pit. "Potatoes? You would actually eat a raw potato?"

His grin grew wider. "Oh yeah, but not just one. Watch this."

He stepped into the hole and proceeded to crunch up five whole, raw Irish potatoes—chewed them up and swallowed them! I had known a few dogs that chewed strange things, but I'd never met one that actually *ate* them.

"Hap, at the risk of sounding narrow-minded, I must tell you that this strikes me as unnatural. In fact, it seems weird."

He finished chewing and gave me a puzzled look. "Huh. I can't believe you've never ate potatoes and watermelon."

"That's what I'm trying to tell you. Dogs don't eat that stuff."

"Well, how about tomatoes and okra and squash?"

His question sent a buzz of electricity down my spine, as it suddenly dawned on me that he had just listed *the very items that were growing in Sally May's garden.* It took me a moment to find my voice. "Hap, you're in worse shape than I thought. We need to get you out of here."

"Well, I'm still kind of hungry."

"I don't care. Out!" I gave the big ox a shove. It was like shoving a tree. "Return to the gas tanks, and that's a direct order."

He didn't want to leave, but he did. That's one of the nice things about Labs. They're not mean and sometimes you can reason with them. Two minutes later, we were back at the gas tanks and I had succeeded in getting the big lug into bed. Only then could I relax.

I did the Three Turns Maneuver and flopped down on my gunny sack. I noticed that Hap was still sitting up. "You're not tired?" He was staring straight ahead and had lost his smile. "What's wrong?"

"I've got an upset stomach."

I didn't want to laugh, but I did. I couldn't help myself. "Of course you have an upset stomach! What did you expect?"

"Do you reckon it was the potatoes? I only ate five of 'em."

"What do you think?"

He looked at me with wooden eyes and nodded his head. "I think maybe it was. And you know what? This has happened before. The last time I ate five potatoes, I got sick."

Again, I had to laugh. "Sorry, pal, I know this isn't funny to you, but when dogs eat food that was never intended for dogs, *they get sick*."

"It seems ridiculous, don't it? I told you, I do ridiculous things."

"You were right, and I even tried to talk you out of it."

He nodded and burped. "I think it's getting worse. Reckon I ought to do something?"

"Well, that's not my decision, Hap, but if I were in your place, I would step outside and

purge my system of watermelon rinds and raw potatoes."

"I think I will. 'Scuse me, I'll be right back."

He hurried out of the office and vanished into the night. Between snickers and chortles, I listened to the sounds of his Flush Procedure (it was loud and rather gross). Once again, I hated to laugh at his misfortune, but...well, it was hilarious. I mean, eating watermelon rinds and raw potatoes! Of all the bonehead things for a dog to do, and this wasn't the first time he'd done it!

In other words, he got exactly what he deserved. Maybe he would learn from the experience.

CHAPTER NINE

Hap Finally Learns a Lesson

He returned five minutes later, and I noticed that he was wearing a sheepish grin. He flopped down on his bed. "I hope the noise didn't bother you."

"Not at all. The question is, did you learn anything from this? I mean, we all make mistakes, Hap, but we need to learn the lessons that Life provides."

His face assumed a serious cast. "I think this might have done it, Hank. Me and raw potatoes have quit being friends."

"That is great news. And let me make one observation that will broaden your experience and put it all into perspective." I leaned toward him and said my words with care. "*Ridiculous actions always produce ridiculous results.* Repeat that."

He pinched his eyes in a show of concentration and said, "Ridiculous produce always gives you a ridiculous belly ache."

"Well, that's close enough. I think you've captured the heart of the core of the apex. Now, can we sleep? When morning comes, I will have a ranch to run."

"Sure. Nighty night." We stretched out on our respective gunny sacks and I was drifting out on the Ocean of Sleep when I heard his voice again. "You know, that lawn mower really fooled me. I would have sworn it was a bull in the yard."

I sat up. "Happy, this hasn't been the greatest night of your life. We need to let it go and forget about it. Go to sleep."

"Yes sir, sorry. I just wanted you to know…"

"Tell me in the morning."

"Yes sir. Nighty night."

"Good night."

Whew! At last he shut his big mouth and we had some peace and quiet. I climbed back into my little rubber raft of sleep and began rowing across the wide Molasses Sea…

"Hank?"

This time, I leaped out of bed, stuck my nose

in his face, and began yelling. "What? What what what what what? What's wrong with you? What do you have against sleep?"

"Well, sorry, I didn't mean to...there's something I need to tell you."

My mind tumbled and I struggled for patience. "All right, tell me—but this is IT. No more talking tonight. What?"

There was a moment of silence. He seemed to be searching for words. "Hank, I'm hungry again."

I hovered over the dark abyss of a total screaming fit, but before I could give him Double Train Horns in the face, I started laughing. "You just threw up and you're hungry again! I don't believe this. Ha ha ha ha." I returned to my bed and collapsed. "Hap, if you wake me up again, I will do something violent and crazy, so don't. Good night."

"Nighty night."

This time, he actually shut his big trap and we both drifted off to sleep. It didn't take me long, about ten seconds. I mean, I was bushed.

You know, this is funny. I had the craziest dream. Ha ha. I dreamed that Big Boy went back to Sally May's garden and ate all her vegetables. Ha ha. Is that crazy or what? They say you have your strangest dreams when you're exhausted. Well, that sure fit.

If I were to tell you that I leaped out of bed at my usual five a.m. and rushed out to bark up the sun, it would be an exaggeration. No, it would be worse than that. It would be a huge whopper of a lie. I slept through my morning chores, and might have slept the rest of the day, only around eight o'clock, I was awakened by a piercing fenimum voice.

Feminium voice.

The piercing voice of a woman, let us say, it was calling my name. "Hank!" I flew out of bed and saw a huge yellow bearskin rug spread out on the office floor. I gave it a three-bark blast and...okay, it was Happy Lab. Remember him?

He didn't stir or even twitch, and went right on sleeping like a dead tree. Isn't that the usual story with sleep-wreckers? They stay up half the night, blabbering and barking at lawn mowers and eating raw potatoes, and then they sleep till noon. Those of us with jobs have to...oh well.

I grumbled, "Relax, pal, I'll take the call. Don't worry about a thing."

With my head still fuzzy with sleep, I headed for the house to see what was going on. I knew *something* was afoot. Sally May doesn't screech my name unless there's some kind of emergency.

About halfway between the office and the house, I met Drover. Apparently he had ventured out of his Secret Sanctuary and...I don't know, was doing something silly with his life. Anyway, we met and he fell in step beside me.

"Hi, Hank. Did you hear that?"

"I heard the voice of Sally May, calling my name. What do we have here? Bring me up to speed."

"Well, I'm not sure. She came out of the house and screeched."

"Drover, I need facts, details. I don't want to walk blind into this meeting. Why did she shriek my name?"

"Well, I don't know. Maybe something scared her."

"I agree. Perhaps she found a snake on the porch, or a lizard. Or a dead mouse. Maybe a mouse tripped over the cat's tail and broke his neck."

"Oh, that was nasty. Hee hee."

"Nasty but true. That's the only way a mouse would ever die on this ranch. Pete's too lazy to catch one."

"Who's that big guy in my bed?"

"What? Oh, him. That's Happy Lab. He got

lost and so-forth, and he'll be our guest for a few days. As you might know, everyone falls in love with a Lab and he gets special treatment. The rest of us are just chopped liver."

"Me too?"

I studied the runt. "Especially you."

"I never cared for the taste of liver."

"Good. Everything works out, doesn't it?"

This is what I have to put up with every day. Sometimes my soul cries out for a few shreds of intelligent conversation, but I start my mornings talking to Drover about chopped liver.

Oh well.

I arrived at the yard gate moments later, with an impressive display of Sirens and Lights. Sally May, Little Alfred, and our local cat were standing on the porch. Alfred wore a peculiar grin, the cat wore his usual annoying smirk, and Sally May... well, her expression was miles away from a grin or a smirk.

She looked mad: flared nostrils, pinched eyes, and both hands jammed against her hips, which always spells trouble.

Drover read the signs and started backing away. "I think it's time for me to leave."

"No, wait. I wouldn't mind having you here to..."

Zoom! He was gone, heading for the machine shed like a bullet shot from a gun. "Coward!" I turned back to Sally May. Okay, what did we have here? Something was wrong...but what?

She told her son (the one with the bratty smile) to open the yard gate. He did, and she said, "Hank, come here."

That was odd. She wanted me to enter her yard, the very place where dogs weren't allowed? I felt uneasy about this, but...well, she'd told me to come, so I went. Lowering my head, I eased through the gate and crept toward the porch. There, I found myself standing face to face with the cat. The very sight of him caused my lips to twitch.

He batted his eyes and purred, "Well, well! We had a busy night last night, didn't we, Hankie?"

"Creep. That wasn't a bull in the yard and you knew it. I ought to..."

"Hank!"

Huh?

"Leave the cat alone."

Yes ma'am, but...

"Come here and look at this."

I pushed my way past the cat (and managed to step on his foot in the process, hee hee) and made my way up to the porch. Sally May's arm, hand, and index finger were pointing like a flaming arrow toward something at the base of the screen door.

She was scowling. "What is *this*?"

I looked closer. Hmmm. It appeared to be a collection of lumpy objects, about seventeen of them. They didn't appear to be snakes, lizards, or mice. I crept closer and gave them a sniffing, then directed a puzzled gaze up to Our Beloved Ranch Wife. Potatoes?

In an icy voice, she said, "Last night, someone moved a whole sack of rotten potatoes from the compost heap, and left them on my porch. *Who did this?*"

My mind raced back to the events of the previous night, and slowly a pattern of clues began to emerge. It all happened after I went to sleep, and I knew exactly who did it.

When something happens that defies explanation, something that's so crazy you can't believe it actually happened, *go find the nearest bird dog*. In other words, this was the handiwork of He Who Doeth Ridiculous Things. But how could I explain it to Sally May?

I gave her Sad Eyes and went to Slow Perplexed Wags on the tail section, as if to say, "Sally May, I know that our relationship has had its ups and downs, but trust me, this is NOT something a cowdog would ever do. We don't deal in potatoes. We never touch them. Honest."

She turned to her son. "Why on earth would a

dog do this?"

He was trying to keep from laughing. "I don't know, Mom, but it sure is funny."

"It's NOT funny." Her eyes came at me like bullets. "Why do you do things like this? First, you bark all night and wake up the whole house, then you drag garbage up on my porch. You are *so dumb*! Alfred, honey, take the potatoes back to the compost, and *you*," she was glaring at me again, "stay out of the compost! And get out of my yard. Scat!"

Yes ma'am. I turned to leave and found myself looking into the grinning face of the cat. Uh oh. Would I be able to resist my savage impulses?

Keep on reading.

CHAPTER TEN

Happy Is Exposed

Pete was snorting and gasping with laughter. For a moment of heartbeats, I gave serious thought to beating the snot out of him, but with Sally May standing nearby and already in a volcanic state of mind, I had to settle for a stinging retort. "Pete, you're despicable."

I tried to step on his tail, but he snatched it away. I hurried out the gate, and there I met... guess who. The World's Happiest Dog. He'd finally dragged himself out of bed and there he was, swinging his tail back and forth and wearing that big Labrador grin that caused women and children to swoon.

I marched straight toward him and gave him both barrels. "I had you tucked in bed. I had you settled for the night, and what did you do? You sneaked out of the barracks and deposited seventeen potatoes on Sally May's porch!"

He seemed surprised by my anger. "Hey, those were good spuds. I thought she might need 'em. Those kids eat a lot of groceries. I was just trying to help, honest."

"The potatoes were sprouting, they were half-rotten, they smelled bad. Sally May didn't want them stinking up her porch."

"Gee, I never thought about that."

"I wouldn't care about any of this, except for the fact that I got blamed for it."

"Are you serious?"

"Look at her face and tell me if I'm serious." I pointed toward the porch and...huh? I couldn't believe this.

She was smiling like the rising sun, and do you know why? Because she had just seen The World's Happiest Dog, and somehow that made her the The World's Happiest Ranch Wife. And here she came down the sidewalk, she and her son, both of them glowing with joy. They brushed right past me and went straight to the Lab, who greeted them with a huge dripping smile.

"Hi, Happy! How are you this morning, huh? Good dog."

Sally May stroked him on the head and Little Alfred climbed on his back and rode him around, laughing and waving his arm as though he were twirling a rope. I even heard him say, "Mom, I wish we could keep him."

Oh brother. I had to stand there and watch. I soon realized that Kitty Kitty had slithered up beside me. He heaved a sigh. "Isn't this sweet?"

My eyes almost bugged out of my head. "Sweet! It's an outrage. It makes me sick. Do you know who dumped the potatoes on the porch?"

"Of course I do. I saw the whole thing." He fluttered his eyelids. "You must find this very discouraging, Hankie."

"You bet I do. If I even have a naughty thought, she sees it. That big oaf can do anything and get by with it."

"I know. It doesn't seem fair, does it?"

"No, it certainly..." I noticed his smirk. "Are you trying to make a mockery of my misfortune?"

His eyes brightened. "You know, Hankie, that does sound like something I might do."

I heard a growl rumbling in the depths of my throat. "How would you like to climb a tree, huh?"

A woman's voice interrupted my thoughts.

"Hank, leave the cat alone!"

You see what I mean? She has radar...FOR ME!

Pete's smirk grew even wider. "Poor doggie! You're not having a good day, are you?"

"Pete, you're disgusting."

I whirled away and left the cat sitting in the rubble of his own shubble. But I had to admit that the little creep had gotten one thing right: I was having a bad day. As a matter of fact, I was beginning to wonder if I might lose my job.

Don't get me wrong. I'd had bad days before, a lot of them, and I had learned to cope with disappointment and injustice, but this was a different kind of problem. How do you compete with a perfect dog? When your people think the mutt can do no wrong, what's left for rest of us who...well, have a naughty thought every now and then, and occasionally mess up?

You can't win. You're wrong from the start, guilty before you're even charged, because it's impossible to compete with someone's dream-notion of The Perfect Dog.

Yes, it was very discouraging. With the sounds of their laughter and happiness echoing through the gloomy, torch-lit dungeon of my mind, I left the scene and trudged back to my miserable, lonely little office beneath the gas tanks. There, I planned to sit on my stinking, flea-infested gunny sack, and spend the rest of my day—or maybe the rest of my life—eating my heart out with a plastic spoon.

Does that sound like a festival of self-pity? Maybe so, and I didn't care. By George, I had earned the right to feel sorry for myself, and that's exactly what I intended to do.

I had been brooding for about ten minutes, when I heard voices and footsteps. I rose and gazed off to the east, and saw Alfred, Sally May, and Happy Lab. They were walking down the hill, and Alfred was carrying the red plastic bucket. It appeared that they were heading for the garden, perhaps to return the potatoes to the compost heap.

They were enjoying themselves, laughing and tossing a stick for the Lab to fetch, a scene of happy people enjoying the company of the Dog of Their Dreams—a dog that wasn't me.

I watched. Alfred reached the open gate. He walked inside the garden, while his mother tossed the stick for Happy to chase and bring back. (Labs are great fetchers). Alfred dumped the potatoes back into the compost and was about to leave...when he froze and looked around the garden.

I heard his voice. "Mom, something got into the garden and ate all the tomatoes. And the squash is gone. And look at the okra plants."

Sally May rushed through the gate. Her eyes grew wide and, even at a distance, I could hear her gasp. "My garden! What...who..." She whirled around and looked in all directions. Then her voice shattered the morning calm. "HANK! If I ever get my hands on that dog...Hank!"

The sound of my name sent a shiver down my spine, and on instinct, I pulled my tail up between my legs. Good grief, I was in trouble again, and I hadn't done anything! I had just about decided to make a dash for the machine shed, when I heard Alfred's voice again.

"Mom, it wasn't Hank. Look at the footprints. They're huge."

There was a long moment of silence. Then Sally May said, "Oh no, surely not. I can't...there must be some...he would never do that, I'm sure he wouldn't."

"Mom, it was Happy."

"But why would he... Do you think he eats tomatoes and squash? That's ridiculous."

"Those aren't coon tracks, Mom. And you know what? I bet he's the one that carried the potatoes up to the house, too."

"Oh my stars! I can't believe this." With a stricken look on her face, she turned around to her precious Labrador...and guess what he was doing. He had found a rake leaning against the fence and was in the process of chewing the wooden handle. That got her attention. "Happy, no! Bad dog! Don't chew my rake."

She made a dive for the rake and...what do you know, Mister Perfect took off, dragging the rake along with him. "Happy! Give me that rake!"

I could hardly conceal my...that is, I was filled with feelings of shock and dismay. I mean, the guy had obviously spent half the night wrecking her garden, and now he was trying to chew her rake into splinters. How tee hee disappointing!

Well! What an interesting turn of events. Someone besides ME had nudged the Lady of the House into a thermonuclear moment. And make no mistake, she was mad. She came boiling out the garden gate and headed down to the corrals to find her husband.

"Loper! Where are you? You need to do something with this dog before he destroys the ranch!"

Alfred stayed behind with Happy and looked

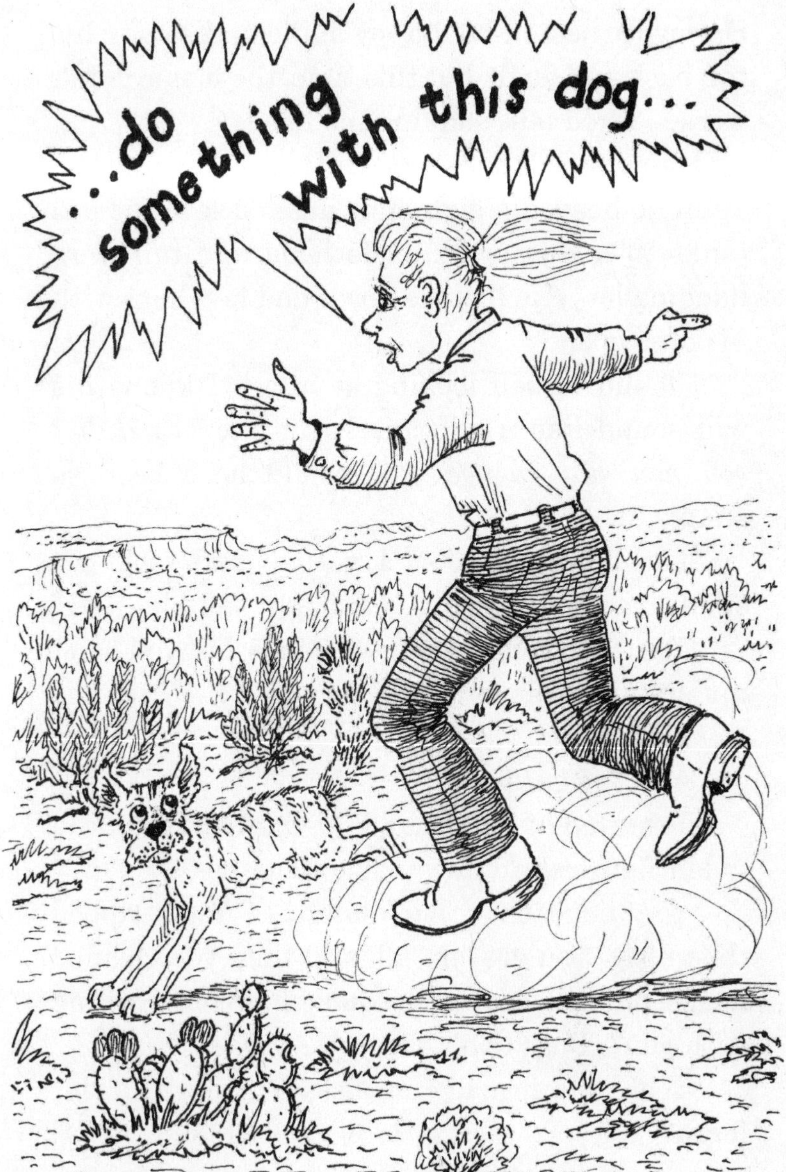
...do something with this dog...

into his eyes. "Why'd you have to go and do that?" Happy turned on his happy smile and swung his tail back and forth, but this time, the magic didn't work. Alfred left, shaking his head.

Happy stood there for a while, looking confused. Then he heaved a sigh and came back to the gas tanks in a slow walk. His head and tail were hanging low. He flopped down and lay there with his eyes open.

I found myself looking at him. "I know this will sound like a silly question, but *why didn't you just stay in bed?* It would have been so simple."

"I couldn't sleep, so I got up and took her spuds back to the house. I thought she'd be glad."

"Yes, well, you're great with kids, but you don't understand women at all."

"I guess not."

"And the garden?"

He stared at the ground. "I wanted a snack. I didn't figure she'd miss a few tomatoes."

"You didn't eat *a few tomatoes*. You stripped the vines. You ate 'em all, and then you cleaned house on the okra and squash! What's wrong with you? Dogs don't eat that stuff!"

"Yeah, and it made me sick. When will I ever learn?"

"Oh brother! What about the rake?"

He shrugged. "I'd never chewed a rake before, and all at once, it seemed like a good idea. I think I really messed up this time."

I stared into his innocent, empty bird-brain eyes. "No, it's worse than that. Normal dogs mess up. I mess up. You have performed a miracle in reverse."

"I told you, I do ridiculous things."

"Yes, well, I had no idea."

"I wrote a song about it. You want to hear it?"

"A song? No thanks, I'm a very busy dog."

"It tells my story. It's about doing ridiculous things."

I heaved a weary sigh and sat down. "Okay, let's hear it."

In case you're interested, here's the song.

CHAPTER ELEVEN

Happy's Confession

Ridiculous Things

I used to think I was a perfect dog,
And I was…for about a month.
Something happened in my childhood
That gave my life a bump.

It started when the paper boy delivered *The Globe*
On the porch right after dawn.
I didn't try to read the morning news.
I chewed it up and spread it on the lawn.

I get tired…of doing things.
That are ridiculous…and strange.

Shredding papers in the yard will lose you
    friends.
Some day I'll need to change.

When my master came out to get his paper
And saw confetti on the grass with the dew.
He screamed at me and his eyes bugged out,
And he tried to drill me with his shoe.

It was a house shoe made of sheepskin.
The real thing, a genuine prize.
I grabbed it and headed down the sidewalk.
He wasn't fast enough to catch me, but he
    tried.

I get tired...of doing things.
That are ridiculous...and strange.
When we steal their shoes, it makes 'em mad.
Some day I'll need to change.

So I found myself at the end of the block,
Wondering what I should do.
I had beat the boss in a foot race
And there I was, alone with his shoe.

Like I said, it was made of sheepskin,
Smelled so good, it gave me fits.

All at once I felt a compulsion
To chew it up in tiny little bits.

I get tired...of doing things.
That are ridiculous...and strange.
When he found the shoe, I was in the stew.
Some day I'll need to change.

I get so tired of doing things that are
    ridiculous.
It really bugs me 'cause I know that it's
    strange.
Eating papers and slippers is totally weird.
Some day I need to think about a change.

Some day I need to think about a change.

Some day I need to think about...chewing
    things, 'cause I love it!

When he finished the song, we both sat in
silence for a while. His happy smile had vanished.
I said, "That's a true story? You actually did
those things?" He nodded. I laid a paw on his
shoulder. "Hap, I admire your honesty, I really
do, and if you're ever out this way again, I hope
you'll stop by for a visit."

"You think I ought to be moving along?"

"No question about it. I'll walk you to the road." We walked in silence to the county road. "Hap, thanks for dropping by, and I hope you have a nice trip."

"Thanks a lot for trying to help. I know you're disappointed in me and I wish..." His voice cracked and he wasn't able to finish his sentence. He turned toward the west and walked away—the picture of a broken dog.

I know what you're thinking. I should have called him back. I should have given him one more chance. I should have...what should I have done? Be fair and honest about this. I mean, there's no law that says a dog can't do ridiculous things, but actions have consequences, right? When we mess up, somebody has to pay the bill. I had my own problems to worry about.

I know, I know. The guy was kind and gentle, likeable, loveable, and great with kids, but he was his own worst enemy. If we let him hang around for another day, there was no telling what kind of disaster he would bring to the ranch. And guess who might get blamed: me.

No, he'd made the right decision: leave the ranch and take his problems down the road. In the long run, everyone would be happier and better off. He would find a whole new set of friends and, for a few hours, they would think he was the World's Most Perfect Dog...until they got the bad news that he was just another lunatic bird dog.

Okay, I'll admit that it made me sad to sit there and watch him trudging off to his next fiasco, but in my line of work, we have to keep a tight rein on our emotions. See, those emotions cloud your mind and lead you into bad...

"Happy? Wait."

I couldn't believe I was doing this. I COULD NOT BELIEVE IT! It went against everything in my background and training. Do you know why I did it? Here's the truth: *Nobody wants to live in a world where Labrador retrievers quit smiling,* and that applies even to hard-boiled Heads of Ranch Security.

Oh brother.

I caught up with him. "Happy, you can't leave."

He gave me a puzzled look. "But I thought you said..."

"Don't tell me what I said. I'm already confused enough. You can't leave, period. You've made a mess of things here, but at least you're safe. Maybe your people will show up to claim you."

"Oh, that would be nice. I sure miss 'em."

"Come with me. You're under house arrest." We started back to the office. "Now listen, you meathead, things have got to change, starting right now."

"Yes sir."

"Stay out of the garden. Stay out of the compost heap. No barking at night, and I don't care if you see the Creature From the Black Latrine. No barking!"

"Yes sir."

"Don't chew the rake. Don't shred paper. Don't tip over the garbage barrels. If you get hungry in the night, eat your heart out. Chew your paw. No more ridiculous behavior. Do you copy?"

"Yes sir, I hear you. And I sure appreciate all your kindness."

I gave him a flaming glare. "It's not kindness, Happy. I know that if you left, I wouldn't be able to sleep for a week. It's purely selfish."

"Well, thanks for all your selfishness."

I couldn't decide whether to laugh or scream in his face, so I let it pass. It was a pretty funny line, actually, "Thanks for all your selfishness." What kind of dog would make such a ridiculous statement? A happy Lab.

We had just about reached the office, when I heard a vehicle coming into ranch headquarters. "Hap, we've got an unidentified vehicle on the ranch and I have to check it out. Go to your room and lie down. Don't do anything until I get back."

"Yes sir."

I didn't leave until I saw him flop down on his gunny sack. Whew! Maybe he would be safe for a few minutes. Then I turned my attention to the approaching vehicle, a pickup with Slim Chance at the wheel. And he was driving faster than normal. I had a feeling that he was bringing some bad news. I was right.

He pulled up behind the house and got out of the pickup. Loper and Sally May were standing beside the yard gate. Loper growled, "What did you tear up this time?"

"We're out of water in the northwest pasture. The wind hasn't blown in three days and the stock tank's down to mud and moss. Cows are standing on their heads, trying to get a drink."

Loper scowled and shook his head. "If it's not one thing, it's another. Well, let's hook up the gas engine. You'll have to camp out and keep it running all night."

A broad smile flashed across Sally May's face.

"He's going to camp at the windmill? I have a wonderful idea. He can take Happy!"

Slim studied her face. "Is there something I don't know?"

Loper filled him in about all our adventures with Happy Lab. He'd barked half the night at the lawn mower, eaten everything in the garden, and tried to eat Sally May's rake. "I put an ad on the radio and surely the owners will show up, but in the meantime, he's a hazard to the ranch."

Slim nodded. "I'll take him. Where I'm going, there won't be anything for him to tear up—unless he chews windmill towers."

Sally May said, "Don't be too sure that he won't. He ate every squash and tomato in my garden, and he needs to go back where he came from."

Okay, it was back to work for me. Windmills are a vital part of the operation of this ranch and Slim would need my help. Most of your ordinary mutts don't know beans about pasture water and windmills. Me? I make a hand.

It took the men an hour to gather up all their windmill tools and Slim's camping supplies, then we headed north in two pickups. (Loper had to help Slim rig up the gasoline pump on the windmill, but didn't plan to camp out, so he took his own vehicle).

Happy and I rode in the back of Slim's pickup, and the Lab seemed thrilled to be going out on a big adventure. "Boy, this'll be fun. I sure appreciate you letting me tag along."

"It won't be fun, Hap. They're putting you on ice, so to speak, taking you to a place where you can't possibly get into trouble."

"Oh, good. That's just what I need. I sure hate to be a burden"

He hated to be a burden. Oh brother. But like I said before, who can stay mad at a Lab? He was the nicest ranch-wrecking dog I'd ever met.

We drove two miles north of headquarters, until we came to an old wooden windmill sitting all by itself on a wind-swept hill, only the hill hadn't been wind-swept in several days, and that was the problem. As Slim had reported, the windmill had quit pumping and the water level in the stock tank had shrunk down to five inches of moss and black stinking mud.

The cattle needed fresh water and that was the whole point of this operation, don't you see, hooking up a gasoline engine to the pump rod, so that it would make a continuous stream of water, whether the wind was blowing or not.

All Slim had to do was wake up four or five

times in the night to fill the fuel tank with gasoline, and I had every reason to suppose that he would need my help. I mean, let's be honest about this. The guy sleeps like a pile of lumber. I needed to be there to make sure he woke up every time the motor ran out of gas. It wouldn't be a glamorous job, but somebody had to do it.

Around four o'clock, the men had bolted the motor in place, hooked it up to the pump rod, and filled it with gas. Hey, they had even checked the oil, which isn't necessarily something you expect your average cowboy to do. Slim grinned, rubbed his hands together, stepped up to the pull-rope, and gave it a crank.

Two hours later, after they had scraped all the sludge and mud dauber nests out of the carburetor, and had screamed themselves hoarse, the engine fired up and went to pumping. Our cowboy crew had won a major victory over the evil gremlins that play nasty tricks on gasoline engines, and they were proud of themselves.

Loper wished us good night and drove back to headquarters, and we prepared for our night on the prairie.

You'll never guess what happened. Never.

CHAPTER TWELVE

Incredible

Slim built a little fire out of cottonwood limbs and started his cowboy supper: bacon, fried potatoes, and canned hash, all thrown together in a big cast iron skillet. As you might expect, I watched this with more than casual interest, and so did Mister Hungry All The Time.

I could hear him slobbering and licking his chops. "Boy, it smells good, don't it?"

"Don't torture yourself, pal. He's not going to share it with us, and even if he did, you'd be sorry."

"Reckon?"

"Oh yes, I've been down this road. He's a bachelor. Anything he cooks in a skillet will give you the most incredible indigestion of your life."

He mopped his lips with his tongue. "I'd sure like to try it. You know about me and spuds. I love 'em."

"It'll never happen."

So we sat there like stumps and watched Slim eat. It was painful. I knew his bachelor food wouldn't taste as good as it smelled, but let's face it, anything cooked with bacon grease smells pretty yummy. You could cook an old tire in bacon grease and it would smell good.

We stared and licked our chops and whapped our tails on the ground, but you know Slim. He takes hints like a buffalo.

But then, wonder of wonders, he looked around and saw us. "Y'all hungry?"

Happy moved his front paws up and down and let out a groan. I tried to be more professional about it. I, well, moved my front paws up and down and let out a groan.

Slim glanced down into the skillet. "Well, I guess you can have what's left. A man ought to share with his dogs."

Exactly right, yes, and it had taken him long enough to reach such an obvious moral decision.

He scraped what was left in the skillet out on the grass. Happy leaped to his feet and stared at it with blazing eyes. "What's the drill here? Can we start eating?"

"Yes, but remember that this will be a Sharing Experience. We'll split everything fifty-fifty."

"Got it."

I was maybe half a step behind him, and by the time I got there, he had vaporized the food. I couldn't believe my eyes. "Hey, you ate it all!"

"I did?" He squinted down at the greasy spot in the grass. "Boy, I sure did. I don't know how that happened."

"It's not a mystery. You eat like a vacuum sweeper."

His eyes turned sad. "I'm sorry, I really am. I guess I'll just go to bed and try to stay out of everybody's way."

"Good idea." He found himself a grassy spot about fifteen feet from Slim's bedroll and flopped down, but I noticed that he didn't stretch out. He was still sitting up. "Now what?"

"I'm still hungry."

"Too bad! Chew a stick. Good night."

And so it was that we began our night on the prairie. The pump motor chugged along for three hours and ran out of gas. Slim woke up, found his glasses beside his bedroll, switched on his flashlight, filled the tank, cranked the motor again, and returned to his bedroll.

He repeated the process throughout the night, and I was amazed that everything worked so well. Slim didn't need me to bark him out of bed, Happy Lab didn't make a peep all night long, and I got a good night's sleep.

I had no idea we had a problem until...well, it must have been around eight o'clock. We'd slept late and the sun was already up, and I heard a croaky voice say, "Where are my glasses? I put 'em right here."

I sat up, blinked my eyes, and glanced around. The pump motor had run out of gas. Happy Lab was curled up in a ball and sending up a long line of Z's. Slim Chance was on his hands and knees, squinting at the ground and patting around with his hand—looking for his glasses.

It took me about five seconds to put this all together, and it hit me like a fat duck falling out of the sky. I leaped to my feet and stormed over to Happy Lab. "Wake up. What did you do with Slim's glasses?"

He staggered to his feet and took a few stumbling steps. "Is it dinner time?"

"No. Where are the glasses?"

"Hey, I just woke up. What are you talking about?"

"Slim left his glasses beside his bedroll.

They're gone and I know you took them."

He stared at me. "Those were his glasses?"

"I knew it! Yes, they were his glasses, and he's half-blind without them. Who's going to drive us back to headquarters?"

"Gosh, I never thought of that."

"What did you do with the glasses?"

"Well, I got hungry in the night."

A cold chill swept over me. "No. You didn't eat them. Tell me you didn't eat a pair of glasses."

"Well, I couldn't find a stick to chew."

I stuck my nose in his face. "Happy, listen to me. No dog in this world is dumb enough to chew up and swallow a pair of glasses. Maybe you gnawed them. Is that what you're telling me?"

He glanced around and shrugged. "No, I ate 'em."

I was stunned. "Nobody eats glasses!"

"Well, I did, but they came right back up, kind of made me sick."

For a long moment, I wavered between an explosion of anger and a fit of insane laughter. *"You ate his glasses and then threw up?"* He gave his head a mournful nod. "Oh brother, this is the craziest..."

Just then, I became aware of Slim's presence towering over us. His hands were resting on his hips and he was beaming a hostile, near-sighted glare down at the Labrador.

He, too, had solved the mystery. "Happy, if you don't find my glasses, you ain't going to be near as happy as you used to be. Where'd you put 'em?"

Squirming with guilt and wagging his tree-limb tail, Hap led us over to the base of the windmill tower. There, in the buffalo grass, we saw a puddle that consisted of bacon grease, fried potatoes, and hash, with Slim's bent-up, twisted wire-rimmed glasses swimming in the middle of it.

Slim bowed his head and mumbled, "They don't pay me enough for this job."

What followed wasn't pretty. With one finger and his thumb, Slim fished the glasses out of the glop and washed them off in the stock tank. He spent a few minutes trying to bend them back into shape, and when he put them on his nose, he looked...well, he looked pretty silly. They were twisted and cockeyed, but at least he could see well enough to drive us back to headquarters.

He gassed up the pump motor and got it running again, and told us dogs to load into the back of the pickup. Through his crooked glasses, he scowled at Happy and grumbled, "Pooch, it's time for you to go home. You've wore out your welcome around here."

On the drive back to headquarters, Happy seemed tormented by guilt. "Hank, I feel awful about this, I really do."

"I know you do, Hap, and I guess you can't help it. But tell me one thing. How did you swallow a pair of glasses? I've never heard of a dog doing that."

He gazed up at the sky. "Well, they sure scraped going down, and I had an uneasy feeling about it right away."

He swallowed a pair of glasses. They scraped going down and gave him an uneasy feeling.

What can you say? Nothing. The spear of anger blunts itself on the rock of truth.

And that's about the end of the story. Against incredible odds, Happy Lab went from being the dog of everyone's dreams, to the dog everyone couldn't wait to get rid of.

And you know what? It worked out slick, because guess who had just pulled up to the house when we got there?

Hap's family, David and Sandra Sell from Booker. They'd heard Loper's ad on the radio and the whole family was lined up and waiting for us when we pulled in: mom and dad and six kids, and they wore the biggest smiles you ever saw in your life.

Happy ran to them and they swarmed all over him, hugging and laughing and squealing with joy. They loved that mutt, absolutely loved him. Beaming a smile, Mrs. Sell turned to Sally May. "Thank you so much for taking care of him. He is the sweetest dog we've ever had."

"Have you had him long?"

"Well, no. Some friends gave him to us two weeks ago."

Sally May nodded. "Do you have a garden?"

"No, we didn't get it planted this year."

Sally May gave her a frozen smile. Slim adjusted his crippled glasses and looked away. Loper coughed and shuffled his feet and managed to say, "Well, we sure enjoyed your dog."

Me? I laughed for three days. Happy Lab, the World's Most Perfect Dog, had ended up making me look like a bouquet of roses, and even Sally May took notice. She apologized for accusing me of terrible crimes and—get this—the next time she went to town, she brought back a package of pig ears for me to chew on.

Wow. Does it get any better than that? Not on this ranch.

This case is closed.

Have you read all
of Hank's adventures?

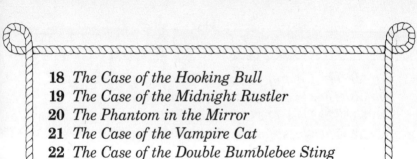

☐ Yes I want to join Hank's Security Force. Enclosed is $12.99 ($7.99 + $5.00 for shipping and handling) for my **two-year membership**. [Make check payable to Maverick Books.]

Which book would you like to receive in your Welcome Package? (#   ) any book except #50

                                                     BOY or GIRL

YOUR NAME   (CIRCLE ONE)

MAILING ADDRESS

CITY   STATE   ZIP

TELEPHONE   BIRTH DATE

E-MAIL   (required for digital Hank Times)

Send check or money order for $12.99 to:

Hank's Security Force
Maverick Books
PO Box 549
Perryton, Texas 79070

DO NOT SEND CASH. NO CREDIT CARDS ACCEPTED.
Allow 2–3 weeks for delivery.
Offer is subject to change.

The following activities are samples from *The Hank Times*, the official newspaper of Hank's Security Force. Do not write on these pages unless this is your book. Even then, why not just find a scrap of paper?

For more games and activities like these, be sure to check out Hank's official website at **www.hankthecowdog.com**!

"Photogenic" Memory Quiz

We all know that Hank has a "photogenic" memory—being aware of your surroundings is an important quality for a Head of Ranch Security. Now you can test your powers of observation.

How good is your memory? Look at the illustration on page 86 and try to remember as many things about it as possible. Then turn back to this page and see how many questions you can answer.

1. How many boards were on the fence? 1, 2, or 3?

2. Could you see HANK'S tail?

3. How many tears did Happy have? 1, 2, or 3?

4. How many boards were on the fence? 2, 3, or 4?

5. Was Hank looking to HIS LEFT or RIGHT?

6. How many of Hank's feet could you see? 1, 2, 3, or all 5?

"Rhyme Time"

I f Happy the Perfect Dog leaves the ranch and looks for a new line of work, what kind of jobs could he do?

Make a rhyme using the name HAP (for Happy) that would relate to Hap's new job possibilities below.

1. Hap makes a special kind of baseball hat.

2. Hap runs a day care center and has kids take this in the afternoon.

3. Hap teaches baby birds to fly.

4. Hap replaces zippers with this.

5. Hap invents a better way to catch mice.

6. Hap makes this to help people get where they're going.

7. Hap does this to get presents ready.

8. Hap becomes a cheerleader and get fans to do this.

9. Hap has a dance studio and teaches this special dance.

Answers:

1. Hap CAP
2. Hap NAP
3. Hap FLAP
4. Hap SNAP
5. Hap TRAP
6. Hap MAP
7. Hap WRAP
8. Hap CLAP
9. Hap TAP

John R. Erickson, a former cowboy, has written numerous books for both children and adults and is best known for his acclaimed *Hank the Cowdog* series. He lives and works on his ranch in Perryton, Texas, with his family.

Gerald L. Holmes has illustrated numerous cartoons and textbooks in addition to the *Hank the Cowdog* series. He lives in Perryton, Texas.